The
Breaking
Words

The
Breaking
Words

Gilaine E. Mitchell

Cormorant Books

 **Canada Council for the Arts** **Conseil des Arts du Canada**  ONTARIO ARTS COUNCIL CONSEIL DES ARTS DE L'ONTARIO an Ontario government agency un organisme du gouvernement de l'Ontario

 Canadian Heritage Patrimoine canadien  Canadä

The publisher gratefully acknowledges the support of the Canada Council for the Arts and the
Ontario Arts Council for its publishing program. We acknowledge the financial support of the
Government of Canada through the Canada Book Fund (CBF) for our publishing activities, and
the Government of Ontario through the Ontario Media Development Corporation, an agency
of the Ontario Ministry of Culture, and the Ontario Book Publishing Tax Credit Program.

LIBRARY AND ARCHIVES CANADA CATALOGUING IN PUBLICATION

Mitchell, Gilaine E., author
The breaking words / Gilaine E. Mitchell.

Issued in print and electronic formats.
ISBN 978-1-77086-299-9 (pbk.).— ISBN 978-1-77086-301-9 (mobi).—
ISBN 978-1-77086-300-2 (epub)

1. Title.

PS8576.I8693B74 2015   C813'.6   C2013-903672-5
C2013-903673-3

Printed and bound in Canada.

Interior text design: Tannice Goddard, Soul Oasis Networking
Cover photo and design: angeljohnguerra.com
Printer: Friesens

The interior of this book is printed on 100% post-consumer waste recycled paper.

CORMORANT BOOKS INC.
10 ST. MARY STREET, SUITE 615, TORONTO, ONTARIO, M4Y 1P9
www.cormorantbooks.com

*The publication of this book is dedicated
to the memory of my loving stepfather,
Roger Smith (1937–2011),
who taught me to hang on to the dream even in hard times,
especially during the hard times.*

ONE

THERE IS A SMALL bank at the corner of Front and Henry in Stirling where Natha commits financial adultery. Her weekly deposits of cash are split, two-thirds into the chequing account, from which she pays the bills, the other third into her savings account, which she calls the "Come What May Account." Devon, Natha's husband, doesn't know about the Come What May Account. She allows for guilt to rise if it must. She has smothered it before. She is aware that Devon would use words like "wickedness" and "misconduct" if he ever found out. He would throw these words against her, intending them to land harder than punches. She smothers this awareness with the knowledge that it is she who is the family breadwinner, not him.

This morning Devon served up gratitude for breakfast and she aligned herself with his good mood. Afterwards, they sunk into their old, comfortable fit, seated in the living room, Devon with his guitar, playing a tune he's been fooling with since they first got together, "Stacks of Gold."

In the bank, she is sure of the title, but the lyrics are hazy. Devon has changed them so much: they now include words like "guidance" and "lure." The tune has never changed.

There's still the hardware store to go to for light bulbs, The Chocolate Shoppe for Celia's chocolate chip cookies, and the drug store for the pill.

"I love you so fucking much," Devon said. "Still," he emphasized.

The words come like her period, on time and short-lived.

The elderly woman ahead of her checks her purse for the tenth compulsive time. The man behind her coughs, the kind of cough that really isn't necessary, it's just done for something to do.

In the lineup at the bank in Stirling.

Decay settles in. Mindless plaque building on bones and brains. She shifts her weight to her left side.

She can't help but think of the card she bought last week at the new bookstore, really the old bookstore but opened up and renovated with a café now and gift items. The card has a photograph on the front taken by a local photographer who travelled overseas — the back of a woman standing in a lineup at a falafel stand in Bangkok. *God favours the brave* tattooed across her back, arcing between her shoulder blades, a hemp leaf above the words, at the base of her neck. She keeps the card in a drawer in her desk and wonders if she'll have occasion to send it to anyone.

What became of the woman in the lineup at the falafel stand in Bangkok? After the picture was taken? Did she walk out of the photographer's range? Where did she go?

Natha could make it all about a life passing — the woman's in Bangkok and her own — but these thoughts don't comfort her. She is comforted by the knowledge that Celia is in school, she is safe. The bills will be paid. Her private account has grown to a healthy sum. She straightens, pushing her shoulders back, feeling a restrained achievement. Her job is not for the lymphatic of souls.

Part of her addiction to money is the process of getting the substance. When the currency is passed to her, a time clock goes off in her head, before the dark-room sex begins; she knows that she will be fed whatever her heart desires. She will have the money. None of the bottom-of-the-list of her youth with Ray and Irene Cole as parents. Her brother Jimmy J. — James John — always got the new pair of jeans they both should have had, Natha stuck in a pair of floods, which announced "Outgrown and Outdated" wherever she went in Stirling. She walked tall just the same; she wasn't stupid or needy.

As long as you're not stupid or needy, she thinks.

The elderly woman ahead of Natha at the bank is talking to the teller now, her thoroughly investigated purse safely on the counter beside her.

Why is there only one turtle-slow teller working?

Natha is impatient with the incompetent teller and fidgets with her long, dark hair. Devon tied it back this morning before she left to run errands. He ties her hair back, he does the laundry and cooks dinner half the time. She doesn't feel obliged to thank him constantly. His part-time job at the garage allows for it. He also massages the knot on the left side of her back near her shoulder, trigger-pointing it into something bearable. He leans into it with his elbow until it hurts and tells her to breathe. The pain never goes away completely; she considers it part of her body now.

The elderly woman and her purse leave and she walks up to the counter with her envelope.

No one in the bank asks where the cash comes from. This one doesn't either.

"Another deposit, Natha?" She pronounces it Nah-tha.

"It's Natha with a long *ā*," she corrects her.

"Sorry," the teller says. "I don't know what it is. I always get it wrong, don't I?"

Christ, Natha thinks. Still. *Nātha,* she used to write on her papers at the beginning of every school year so the bloody teachers would get it right. She was supposed to be a Nathan, Daddy even bet on it with the farmers who used to come in and hang around the feed mill where he worked, chugging his rye, another son about to be born. So her mother has told her countless times, recalling how she was quick on the ball to clean up the mess by naming her Natha, as close to Nathan as you can get.

"Will you be wanting that divided between your two accounts, as usual?"

They know how she banks. Some even chat her up, or joke, Did you rob another bank? Fishing. Fishing. Doris, the one who's been there forever, with her pointy chin and serious brow, once said, "Cash! So much cash. No one ever deals in cash anymore." Natha was in a good mood and answered that she buys and sells antiques and just won't deal any other way.

She had just seen an auction listing in the local paper and thought she'd use that story to put Doris's curiosity to an end. Since then, Doris always asks, "What antiques do you have for sale these days?"

This other teller, the turtle, counts the money several times. She and the rest of them would die if they knew. She could easily have had sex with any of their husbands, or sons or fathers. And here she stands with a stiffened back to guard against anything they might know or suspect about her, depositing her tax-free money because her clients can't stand to be in a sexless marriage anymore, or are widowed and don't want a complicated relationship. Or. She doesn't work Stirling, not since those years with Jules Moore, the original bookstore owner, before he got too needy. She knows better than that in a town where people notice everything.

"Your receipt, Ms. Cole."

Banking done, she crosses the street in this place she has lived all her life. A quaint old town that can even lay claim to great theatre, now that the building has been restored and attracts actors and directors from Toronto and Stratford. It's a simple enough town with a few restaurants, Stedman's department store, speciality shops, and five churches as well as a Jehovah's Witness Hall, all of them spread along the main streets. There are apartment buildings in the west end, and one behind the liquor store in the north end, not far from the legion and the lumberyard. The tallest structure is the water tower, painted light green, which is near the cemetery. Most of the storefronts on Mill Street and Front Street have been changed to make the town look even older. The odd one has an awning or has been freshly painted in dark red, or an intense green. There's one grocery store. And, in a town that prides itself on hockey, there's a large arena that sits in the west end, near the fairgrounds.

The wooden floor at the hardware store is still scuffed from the generations of men searching for nuts and nails and the perfect solution to unclog the toilet. Natha is suddenly annoyed when she passes the handyman brochures, pissed with the fact Devon hasn't started the deck she wants in the backyard. If she knew which nails were needed, she'd buy them and make a bed of thorns just to get him going. But she has left the building of the deck in his procrastinating hands. In the light bulb section she feels her frustration building into a sunburst of pain in her back, under her left shoulder.

She drops her shoulders for relief.

Will the deck ever get built?

And what will she do with her six-year-old all summer?

Celia will have arts and craft days. There'll be picnics at King's Mill and days of relief from the heat at her mother's cottage on Oak Lake. That relief will not be pure. She'll be subjected to Irene's drinking and resulting shrinking ability to converse intelligently.

Natha remembers now, she's supposed to see Irene today.

She'll go to Stedman's — not today but one day soon — for socks and buttons. She'll teach Celia how to make puppets out of socks — wool for the hair — and she'll store them in her closet until summer and pick a rainy day when Celia is bored. "Mr. and Mrs. Sock," they will call them. Natha will make up stories.

Something about trust.

In her own childhood, she did trust her mother, Irene. She trusted her to make dinner every night and she trusted that Daddy would go to work every day and she trusted that her clothes would be washed, dried, and folded — until the day Irene deemed her old enough to do it herself. And that's when Natha's trust shifted. When she was ten and dinners became erratic or ignored altogether and Daddy often missed work Monday mornings and stayed in bed or vomited in the bathroom.

Celia will always be fed.

Natha misses her during the day and wants her to be here in the hardware store shopping with her, filling little brown bags with nails or screws, handing the money to the cashier, keeping the change for bubble gum. Anxiety sets in when Celia is at school; she feels threatened by their separation. It is not enough to be around Devon. Natha frequently enters Celia's bedroom to alleviate a sense of growing despair; she hates that her life comes down to the presence of bodies. Or the absence of them.

In the midst of her anxiety, with the beating pain of the knot in her back, she finds herself at the cashier, paying, putting the change in her change purse, arranging the bills in her wallet from smallest to largest. She's holding up another customer. Arnie, a stout man with a large stomach, is patient. She stopped hurrying to get out of the way of others when she was ten, that age when everything seemed to change. Her mother's dedication to the family, Daddy's work ethic, the bloom of her own awareness that she could stand in a room with two people screaming and the world would go on without her. Today is Wednesday, June fourth, she reminds herself.

She has only recently decided every day should be noted — the day of the week, the month, the day of the month. It's a sudden habit, a reaction to not being able to recall certain times in her life, in her childhood and youth, even the middle years of her marriage, before Celia came along, as if calendars didn't exist before her birth, and really, up until now, didn't exist at all, and now it seems vital that she recognize the date out loud like the clapboard before filming starts.

The thing about the early days of June is that they feel early, the early on of something. Yet it bugs her that she's thinking ahead; she stops herself. *These are the good days*, she thinks. She's had her bad times and whatever fell before them were good in comparison. She can only go through her days now, thankful they're not so bad. And, in comparison to what might come, they are good. She fastens to this thought as she makes her way to The Chocolate Shoppe, thinks briefly about dropping in to see her one and only friend, Ruthie, the same age as her mother, who works at the library, but heads instead to the drugstore and then home to her old red-brick house on Edward Street, which sags slightly to the right. Daddy told her it sags because they built the house on a slight slope and it was a mistake to go with the shape of the earth.

Devon is in the garage when she gets home, fixing the engine on a friend's car. Forever fixing a friend's car for cash or beer or pot. She'd prefer he worked full-time at the Ford dealership instead of just part-time, maybe then she wouldn't have to work so much herself. He's always found reasons not to and she's always accepted them, especially when he said it was so he could spend more time raising Celia, being there as Dad, surely she could understand that, the importance of it, her own Daddy having left when she was fourteen. How could she argue?

"You get the bulbs?" he asks, lifting his head from under the hood. His hands are black, as is a spot under his nose where he no doubt wiped away an itch.

"Of course. Here," she says, handing him the bag.

"The light in here is the shits to begin with," he complains. "Then a bulb goes out and I'm practically in the dark."

His tawny-coloured hair is uncombed and falls around his face in stringy curls, but he is still a good looking man — or guy — as she thinks of him. Lately, she's been seeing more of the boy, the one she imagines he was, wiping his nose as he still does, seems he always has an itch there. He is much taller than she is, lanky; his body moves in jerks as if he's about to pounce on her.

He comes around the side of the car and stands in front of her. She is usually weary when she gets back from the bank, unsure if he'll start quizzing her about how much she put in, what she kept out, how much is there in total. Most of the time he doesn't say a word, the financial part of their lives left in her hands.

But she wonders if he can see her deception. The secrecy of her Come What May Account known only to herself.

"I forgot I'm supposed to be going to my mother's today. Want to come?"

"Too much work to do. Besides, I can't handle your mother today."

"I'm not sure I can either."

He opens the package of bulbs and hands one to her, then climbs onto the roof of the car so he can reach the light fixture hanging above.

"I can tell you're uptight about it," he says.

"I'm not uptight, Devon."

"It's all over your face."

"I doubt that," she replies, handing him the bulb.

"Remember, I can see everything, even though most people can't," he says. "You're agitated."

"I'm fine," she insists.

She lets out a long sigh. She is agitated now at his insistence she's in one state or another, his usual game. He believes he can read her, read everything about her, and tells her so. If she's not careful she ends up believing what he says. Like the time he said she only works with his approval. She was a hooker before she ever met him and told him she'd only ever quit when she was ready to. She believes it sometimes, telling some of her clients that she works with her husband's approval. "Get out," they say. "What kind of man lets his wife fuck other men?" "He must be a lazy dumb fuck."

"Is it that obvious?" she asks Devon, letting him believe in himself.

"To me it is."

More light is shed.

"Well, I said I'd go and I really need a swim."

Devon jumps down and saunters around to the front of the car, leans against the hood.

"Sure," he says, "Walk right into that minefield."

"I'm used to minefields, remember? Every night I work," she snaps back. She almost slams the garage door behind her on the way into the house, the force of her own hand unexpectedly harsh. At least the day had started off well.

THE DIRT ROAD LEADING down to her mother's cottage — really, her year-round house — has just been sprayed with calcium and the smell lies thick under her nose. It's one of summer's smells, Natha thinks, pushing back the bad turn in the conversation with Devon. This morning he loved her "so fucking much," but his insistence on pegging her as agitated has all but wiped those words away.

"Never mind," she says to the full bloom of the birch trees that line the road, this oasis off the highway, south of town, up in the Oak Hills. She can't get used to the monstrous new homes she passes on the way, now that Stirling has become such a desirable place to live, a bedroom community to the city of Belleville a little farther south.

Wednesday, June fourth.

The thing about June, as long as the children are in school, is that it feels too early to call it summer, although today the weather says it is. Natha feels as though she is playing hooky. Come to think of it, every day of her life for the past twenty years has felt like she's been playing hooky, living in opposite time to the rest of the world — the freedom of her days, punching in for work at the Sunrise Motel in Belleville on the nights she has her dates. Celia thinks she's at night school at the local college, studying literature. "What's literature, Mommy?" "What will you be when you graduate?" Celia's questions are harder to navigate than the potholes on the road.

Irene greets Natha with a loose hug — a non-hug — and steers her back outside so she can get back to her drink — beer in a coffee mug — which is sitting on a table between two chairs near the shoreline. Natha hears the sound of boats farther down the lake but can't see them. The forest to the right of her is tall and wide and juts out over the shoreline, trees crooked and stretching over the water.

"Your brother called me last night," Irene says. "Looking for money. No doubt he'll call you, since I turned him down."

"I don't have it this time, Mother."

"He'll try. You can be sure of that."

A couple in a red canoe glides by, synchronized by their paddles. They don't speak.

"Said his line of credit is through the roof."

"I can't help him."

"You never were a worry that way, Natha."

It's the closest her mother ever comes to saying she knows what Natha does for a living. Natha's friend, Ruthie, has a theory that Irene has always known. So does Devon. So does Natha. Since the mention of cleaning houses has long been absent from their conversations, her mother hasn't questioned how she contributes to household expenses.

"I have to go to the bathroom," Irene announces, getting up from her chair, grabbing her mug, which is still half full, and scurrying across the lawn. Natha can hear it, the sound of urine flowing through her tubes. Irene will either come back wet or in a different pair of shorts; which, Natha does not know. It could go either way. How many beers has she had this morning? Whether her mother makes it to the bathroom in time or not, she will come back with another drink either wet in the crotch or freshly changed, the smell of urine only faint.

The scent of the pine and spruce skim Natha's nose, and a slight agitation settles in. Of course, it's beer at ten-thirty in the morning, in a coffee mug, because that means her mother doesn't have a problem. If it weren't for the fact that Irene and her partner Clyde, a retired town clerk, live on the lake, she wouldn't come so often. That, and mostly the fact that Irene let Natha move back into her childhood home — the crooked house on Edward Street — and take over the mortgage when she and Devon wanted out of their cramped apartment above Stedman's. They agreed that if Irene ever wanted to sell the house, they'd split the profit, something Natha has never felt was really fair since Irene made her quit school after grade ten so she could clean houses and help pay the mortgage after Daddy left, when Irene had nothing but the small wage of a waitress at Ren's Restaurant. Natha only agreed because Irene didn't have a problem if Natha didn't have the money occasionally. That hasn't been the case for years now; besides, the mortgage will be paid in another two years.

Irene surprises her by returning with a glass of rye. Time must really be passing, she thinks, it must be eleven o'clock, the witching hour when the hard stuff comes out. No waiting for noon hour for Irene. "Some people eat lunch early," she once said. New shorts too — dark pink ones.

"You know your great aunt Vivian, on your father's side, was entrepreneurial too," she says.

"Yes, you've told me, Mother."

"I don't think I ever told you how enterprising she was."

"I know she made hats. Did she sell them too?"

"Yes, yes. It was her shop. She didn't work for anybody and she'd wear her new creations all around Belleville and stop women in the streets. I tell you, a born entrepreneur."

"I remember Aunt Peggy," Natha says, changing the subject from the enterprising women in the family.

"My mother's sister."

"I remember her story."

"Never married, that one."

"She was cranky and stern."

"You want a beer, or a Caesar?"

"Not now. Maybe later."

"Devoted to the cross, Peggy was."

"A spinster," Natha says.

"There was a man she was in love with when she was younger, but he wasn't Catholic so she turned him away. Worked faithfully for the government employment office for thirty years, wore wool skirts in the winter and pleated polyester in summer and blouses buttoned to the top of her bloody neck where her chosen love hung from a silver chain."

"Jesus on the cross."

"She'd fidget with it when she sat on the white wicker on the screened porch on Saturday afternoons, listening to that godawful opera on the radio. That's what life comes down to when you're married to Jesus Christ."

"Where is Clyde anyway?" Natha asks.

"In town, getting parts to fix the pump. You want a drink now?"

"No. I'm going to go for a swim."

"Suit yourself."

Irene lights a cigarette and hands it to Natha, then lights one for herself. Natha watches her out of the corner of her eye, a tiny woman with short white hair, staring out over the lake, her mouth gaping open as if stuck in the middle of a word she cannot say. When did this start, Natha wonders, this open mouth thing?

"I sure as hell wasn't married to Jesus Christ," she says, the old bitterness swimming around in her mouth with the rye.

"No," Natha says. "You weren't."

Before her mother can get into it, Natha rises out of her chair. "I'm going for a swim now. We'll talk more when I get back."

"Over to the raft?" Irene asks.

"Yes."

"Suit yourself."

NATHA LIKES THAT THE raft is far away, across the lake; swimming to it calls for endurance. She likes that once there, she'll be able to lie in the sun in her bikini on the warm wood, forgetting everything.

She can see a few young women with toddlers on the small beach ahead, at the canteen, a red pail near the shoreline. The sand is coarse there, what sand there is, the beach is mostly grass. She remembers lying on it on a towel while Daddy and Irene drank at a picnic table, their large, white cooler beside them on the ground, the ham sandwiches with relish packed in Baggies, a bag of chips shoved in there too, which became too cold and lost some of its taste.

Irene would only have one drink then.

Irene is shrinking as Natha treads water and looks back. The long ago sound of her mother moaning returns before she turns and swims towards the raft.

A large cloud moves in front of the sun, making it easier on her eyes, easier to see the bodies of the young ones ahead, mothers running after them, the red pail carried by one of them.

Please don't let them know harm in their lives, she thinks.

Is this a prayer?

Not likely. The closest she's ever come to God is that card with the woman in line at the falafel stand in Bangkok with *God favours the brave* tattooed across her shoulders.

Not a prayer, but an utterance to the elements around her.

When she finally arrives at the raft, she lifts herself onto it. She hopes for the quick return of the sun to warm her as she lies there, waiting for it. The giggling screams of the children, the mothers' commanding voices, and the faint sound of a radio calm her. The children wave to her. She waves back, then sets her head back down, and the cloud curtsies out of the way, allowing the sun access to her skin, the many layers of skin that have seen her through to this moment. Married, with a child, working with the approval — no, the insistence of her husband. The insistence of a married life that is different than everyone else's. Right now it sits fine with her, she and Devon being out of sync with the rest of the world, it is okay that she is still married to him, uncommon and dysfunctional as it may be; it is better to her than being common and functional. Anyone can live that story, she thinks.

So she's a hooker. And he has his periodic affairs. At least they don't impose the impossible expectation of fidelity forevermore on each other. Devon has always said their extramarital sex only feeds the marriage. Everything is always about feeding the marriage.

People will bring down whole histories just to fuck someone else, she thinks.

Why lose everything over it?

It makes more sense not to, she believes. Besides, look what happened to her own parents.

"I'm leaving today, after we go fishing," Ray Cole told her that summer day when Natha was fourteen. Plainly. Out of the blue. They were walking down Edward Street towards the Mill Pond. She was thinking of Toronto, of how they were only a couple hours east of it and she'd never been and Daddy said he'd take her that summer, to the Exhibition.

"You won't understand it now, Natha, but she's more like a sister to me than a wife, and you can't live that way for too long."

He pulled out his cigarettes from the front pocket of his short-sleeved shirt, the bulge of too many ryes pushing the buttons over his stomach to the extreme.

"Cigarette, Nat?"

She could easily have been embarrassed by him, by a father like him, by his fat stomach and ruffled black hair that looked like he just woke up no matter how much he combed it back, and pants that had tears in the knee or a rip in the ass. His throat always sounded like it needed clearing. She could have been embarrassed if she hadn't tossed that away in favour of his savvy ways and his vulnerability to her. She alone could destroy him with the wrong look and he confided in her more than he talked to Irene. In fact, they hardly talked at all, mostly yelled under the kitchen ceiling. Natha was his shadow, following him around town as he walked with a slight drag of his left leg, hefting his weight around as if he were the mayor.

Daddy figured big then.

And on that summer day, she took the cigarette from his hand. Ray stopped in his tracks, put one to his own mouth. She took a drag, the intensity of it caught her, leaving her coughing and spitting on the sidewalk. But she continued walking with Ray, smoking her cigarette, to the Mill Pond at the end of the street, past the Presbyterian Church that sits at the corner. She took the odd puff but didn't inhale again. She sensed the need to have one with her father as they walked carrying the sardine sandwiches Ray had made that morning. Sardines with ketchup. He was quieter than usual.

"I don't know how else to explain it, Nat. You just can't live with a wife who feels more like a sister."

The pavement felt wavy, but she walked on. Daddy had once said she was as strong as the big maple out front, and now he was saying, "It's a helluva life, Nat."

"Why?" she asked.

"Because of the sisterly thing. Aren't you listening? Got a job driving truck in Thunder Bay. I'll visit. And I'll call."

He motioned for them to cross the street.

"It's not like you'll never see me again," he said. He put his arm out to block Natha from crossing.

"She's still in bed," he said. "Won't get up. I told her last night."

"I have to pee," Natha said to him. "I'll be back in a minute."
Ray shook his head.

"You still don't know enough to go before you leave."

Had he been the one to teach her how to sit on a toilet?
Or call out for her to go before she went to school?

On the raft, Natha thinks memory is like the water that
lies under the surface of the lake; it laps against the present
moment. It seems her life didn't start until she was ten or
eleven; she can't remember much before then.

She took off that summer day, left Daddy to cross the street
on his own to sit next to Jimmy J. at the water's edge. She was
headed back to the house. She didn't really have to pee. She
was concerned about her mother. Irene was still in bed and
Natha could hear the awful moaning as soon as she stepped
inside. She climbed the stairs past the Rogue's gallery in the
hallways, stopping to look at the family photos which seemed
more important then, staring into the faces of Ray and Irene's
wedding picture, in their early twenties, Ray half smashed. She
could tell by the cocky grin on his face.

I only pretended to pee that morning, she has always wanted
to tell Irene.

She even sat on the toilet and a trickle came out, she took
her time washing her hands. Then Irene's moaning stopped
for a minute and she really did think about going in, but the
moaning started up again. Daddy was waiting for her to do one
last fishing trip. He'd be gone and Mama would still be there.
Why were the moans so much like the sound of a whale?

She stepped out of the bathroom, glanced at her parents'
bedroom door, and then walked out of the house and back,

towards the pond, the place of grander moments — years of fishing with Daddy. She walked slowly, wishing the pond were a lake and not a puddle, a wide open lake with waves. As she pictured this, she imagined whales moaning like Mama. It was a drowning thought, her own private thought that she'd never share with anyone. She had learned the value of her private thoughts when she was fourteen, one morning when Daddy walked by her room when she was getting dressed for school. He was home that day instead of at work at the feed mill because he had a bad hangover. He stood in the doorway and eyed her up and down. She was wearing black bikini underwear and a small white bra. He stood there for the longest time. She felt naked and flushed and wrong.

"You're filling out nicely," he finally said. "Your mother's making pancakes. You'd better hurry up."

She hates remembering that morning.

She hates remembering biting into a sardine sandwich the day Daddy was leaving. She just wanted another cigarette from him and a swallow of his rye which he carried in a flask on their Saturday fishing trips. She made herself cross the street that day, jumping over the guardrail along the road, so that she could sit with Ray and Jimmy J. on their last expedition together.

Now it seems odd that she was thinking of whales. Irene is hardly the size of one. More like the white, fluffy puff of a dandelion gone to seed, curled up in her chair, surrounding the rim of her glass in her circle of inebriation. Natha may have let Daddy win that day, leaving Irene to moan in her pain, but she's here now — thankfully, now on the raft across the lake with only the sounds of the young children.

It could go on — how different things might have been if she had told Irene that Daddy told her about the sisterly thing — but she counts the children and the seagulls trying to pick French fries from their small hands, then tilts her hand above her eyes, blocking out the sun, just blocking.

She breathes, in and out, just like when she swims. Her head is clear; her mind blank.

Until she hears a motorboat approaching; it is like being awakened by the sudden sound of a vacuum when she's struggling for sleep.

It's Devon in the boat, waving. The raft rises and falls with the repeated slaps of water beneath her. A sharpness enters her breath as he makes his way towards her.

Christ, she thinks. So much for solitude.

He shuts the motor off and glides in, smiling and grabbing onto the raft.

"I wanted to swim back," she says impatiently.

"You know your mother. She insisted I get you."

"Oh, for fuck's sake."

She climbs into the boat, pushing yellow rope out the way so she can sit down.

"You don't have to be so pissed about it," he says, his eyes red from smoking pot, she guesses. He starts the motor and pulls away gently. The children start to wave and so she waves back. She is mad for her sudden shift to anger and for saying "fuck" and for the interruption in her tranquility. She was getting there. And all for the sake of her mother's mind, already afloat on a sea of rye, no doubt fantasizing Natha's inability to swim back safely. It's difficult for her to say "I'm fine" when

Devon yells over the sound of the motor, "It's too nice a day to be in a bad mood."

Back at the cottage, she calculates the number of Irene's drinks, how many times she's peed. Clyde, tall and thin and slightly hunched, seems to know a lot about how to fix things; he takes pride laying out the pieces for the pump. She counts them too. The cottage's smells of pine and spruce skim her nose again. She lies when she says it was good after all that Devon drove up and took the boat to bring her back from the raft. The sound of ice cubes in Irene's glass, the comforting familiar sound of something unsettling, settles in her stomach.

In the guest room, Natha takes off her bathing suit and dries herself. She notices a few pairs of shorts piled on the bed. The door opens and Irene walks in.

"You're fit. I'll say that," her mother says, slurring her words, losing her balance, grabbing on to the dresser.

"What are you doing, Mother?"

"These shorts should fit you," she says, pointing to them. "They don't fit me anymore. I haven't worn them in years."

"They're not exactly my style."

"They're good shorts, lots of wear in them yet. Here. Try these white ones on."

"Really, Mother, I'm not interested."

"Try them on." Irene practically shoves them at her. "A new pair that doesn't cost anything."

"I have shorts."

Irene throws them on the bed.

"Oh, yes, I forgot," she says. "You, with all the money in the world can buy everything you want."

"I just don't like them."

"You can at least hurry up and get dressed. I'm putting lunch out."

"I'm getting there."

She sees Irene eyeing her body.

"I didn't have stretch marks either."

Natha picks her underwear up.

"I haven't seen you naked since you were old enough to have a bath by yourself. You always were secretive about your body."

Natha puts her underwear on, fastens her bra.

"Well," she says. "This is what I look like at thirty-five."

Irene walks to the door then turns back.

"You used to call that your 'pee,'" she says, with a thread of disgust in her voice. She leaves the room, closing the door behind her, pulling it tight. Natha finishes dressing. She can't remember her mother giving her baths, can't remember starting to take them on her own. She focuses instead on what Irene has just said and thinks that Irene should have seen her at fifteen when she started having sex with Jules Moore, the widowed bookstore owner, when her vagina began to buy her the freedom to buy the things Irene wouldn't. Irene thought Natha was just cleaning his house. She does remember calling it her pee, the way Celia does now even though Natha has told her it's called a vagina.

This is what my pee looks like now.

Is it good enough, Mother?

That Irene of all people should turn away from what it looks like now.

The thought of sticking around and eating egg salad sandwiches and prolonging her time here is too hard to swallow. Natha steals Devon's drink from his hand, places it on an end table, and leads him to the door. She loads him into the car and drives home, where she takes a shower and gets dressed all over again. Clean, she is; clean, but she can't seem to make love with Devon with the tranquility she briefly felt on the lake. She tidies up Celia's room and then takes a walk along the old railway trail to the east end of town. The word *vagina* strikes her when she arrives back home to the house that has seen the maturation of her body. She succumbs to the agitation she now feels and pours herself a glass of white wine and smokes a few cigarettes. She waits for the end of the school day when she can experience joy again, with the return of her daughter.

THERE IS A CURTAIN she passes through at night before she goes out. She puts Celia to bed as Mother. As she leaves the house and gets into the car, she becomes Sketchy Woman. Later, on the page of a motel bed, she sees herself in charcoal graces. She has drawn herself sitting naked on the edge of a bed, her back to the observer's eye, her buttocks spreading out on the bed. She wrote the word *robotic* beneath this image. The curtain she passes through at home is heavy and deep red with a brocade pattern, dusty now. This is all in her "remarkable mind," as Devon says, although he relies on it every bit as much as she does in order for her to do what it is she does. "It's all those books you've read." That's where he thinks her imaginary curtain comes from: Sylvia Plath and Anaïs Nin and Virginia Woolf and hundreds of others. She tells Celia that these books are her school books.

She slides herself in beside Celia and wraps a leg around Celia's legs — baby chicken legs, as she has called them ever since Celia was a baby. She is thankful to be in her daughter's bed at this moment. Later, it'll be another story.

Celia is tall for her six years, with long legs like her mother. She has Natha's long, dark hair and her pale skin, but her eyes are blue like her father's.

The evening air breezes in through the open window while Celia's blue dolphin lamp adds an embryonic feeling to this time together; it is embryonic in all that will come their way as mother and daughter. Natha has been telling Celia stories from birth, since two a.m. the night Celia was born. She slept in a glass crib until Natha placed her in bed beside herself, the baby poking through the newfound air.

Natha isn't sure what room she'll be in later, or which bed in the liquor- and cigarette-smelling motel. Another guy with another mouth. "Shut up," she'll want to say. "Do you really think you have anything worthwhile to say to me?"

But now, behind the deep red brocade curtain, she sets these thoughts aside and cuddles Celia, her daughter's small form fitting into her own.

Against the pink- and white-striped sheets on Celia's bed, Natha puts her hands together and then opens them up like a book, a handbook she calls them, with stories she makes up as she goes.

Shaggy Bear is tonight's story.

In Natha's open hands, Celia goes to a park with her and

the much-loved Shaggy Bear, a dishevelled looking teddy bear Celia's had forever. At the park there's a younger girl who watches Celia play on the swing and the slide and asks Celia if she can play with Shaggy Bear. What harm will it do?

"It's good to share," Natha tells her. "And the little girl says, peeese, can I play with him?"

Celia giggles.

"Why does she say peeese, Mommy?"

"Because she's so young and doesn't know yet how to say 'please' properly like you do."

"That's funny. 'Peeese,'" she repeats. "Is Daddy at the park?"

"No, just us. Now, you really don't want to give up your bear, but I'm the one holding him while you climb up and down the slide."

"Then what happens?"

Natha feels her muscles twitching in her legs and her arms. Her body feels as if it has fallen asleep, numb and tingling. This is the beginning of the road to her preparation. It is part of it. She struggles to stay concentrated on the rules Celia is setting out for the little girl in the park, how the little girl keeps saying "otay" instead of "okay." Celia giggles, as she always does at this point; she has heard this story before, over and over, and yet she still seems engaged and surprised by it.

The red brocade curtain opens slightly. Variation is on her mind as she employs new words and a new twist to the story.

"I don't mind sharing you," Devon said so many years ago. "As long as I'm home base and our marriage is sacred."

She'll be travelling soon, down the highway. Without any assurance of a happy ending, yet under the safe ceiling of

Celia's room, she feels a strong reluctance in coming to the end of the story. She wants to hold Celia until sleep sets in.

It was believable, Devon's story of how they would live against the rest of the world, in spite of the rest of the world.

Celia rolls over.

"Tickle my back, Mommy," she says quietly.

There's a large black-and-white ultrasound picture of Celia's developing spine in the drawer of the washstand in Natha's room. She didn't ask the technician or the doctor for the sex; she knew her baby was a girl. She'd known she'd have a baby girl with Devon; so, when he asked her to marry him, she said yes.

She hates to part with Celia, now sleeping. Her feet manage to hit the floor.

She stands, leaves her daughter's room, and exits the house, passing through the curtain, to the other side. Her back is stiff. Guarded, she drives into the night.

THE ROOM IS NOT so dirty that she would call it "fleabag." Not so clean that she could call it a suite.

She could use Anaïs Nin now.

He likes that she insists on a dark room and that she has brought a flashlight so he can shine it on her vulva, highlighting it, to make himself erect.

His sex meets hers with a fury. What is there to say about what goes on in these rooms that hasn't been said before?

First, there is the conversation and the drinks.

Then there is the bed.

The smells.

The sounds.

Tonight, some guy named Stin, a glassblower from Picton, married with two children and an inexplicable need to find a metaphor in all of this.

"I work with two furnaces," he says when it's over. "One of them is called the glory hole — well, actually, the hole going into the furnace is called the glory hole, where you insert the glass to reheat and reshape it."

"Right," she says. She does not rush them away. Rushing them pisses them off.

"Well, the way I see it, Natha. You're my glory hole now," he says with a grin. "I'm a different man now," he adds, running a finger down her backside.

"What kind of name is Stin, anyway?"

"Austin. But that has always sounded too rich and pretentious to me."

"So you're a Stin."

"Yes. What kind of name is Natha, anyway?" he mocks her.

"It's a girl name," she answers with slight impatience in her voice. "For a Nathan-boy who never arrived."

"Tell me more."

"How about Chapter Two next time? You do want a next time, don't you?"

She wasn't there the whole time.

She met him at Larry's Bar, sized him up. In fact, she was pleased that he was a rather stunning man with his dark looks. She's into aesthetics as much as anyone. Into them, but not fooled by a man's looks. In keeping with her rules, he was the one to rent the room. He had passed the phone test before she met him. They all have to. No sounding like a psychopath or a girlfriend-searcher. It helps in this case that he knows Stephen, the lawyer, another client. She can trust Stephen not to send her assholes.

She was there the in the bar. But with him now, watching him wipe his penis off with a washcloth so there's nothing for his wife to smell, she feels nothing. She remembers the jabs and the pinching and then it comes back — how long he managed to stay erect; how he told her he can only come by his own hand at forty-three; and how his wife sees this as rejection. But he likes to be inside a woman, and he was staying inside for her and didn't she?

She did come.

Then watched him spill his seed all over her tummy.

The fucker, she thinks.

It rarely happens.

That she comes.

Wednesday, June fourth. It's ten-thirty, the clock on the bedside table displays.

She steps outside the motel room, closing the door, her hair wet from the aftermath shower. A few hours with a guy named Stin. It wasn't so bad. She learned a thing or two about glassblowing — that glass is made from sand.

There's the sex and the money. And then there are the stars to see.

The Nathan-boy part of the conversation idles in her mind as she lights a cigarette and drives out of the motel parking lot, heading north along the strip of fast-food joints and car dealerships, the sign for the Sunrise Motel shrinking in her rear-view mirror.

Christ. Forget it, she tells herself, the smell of the cigarette bringing her back to her car. The cigarette. The steering wheel. The dashboard. The stars guiding her home. No radio. She prefers the sound of her speed and the wind, windows down, her hair flying and drying, as much as it will in the half hour drive from Belleville to Stirling. Small city. Small town. The extent of her geographical life.

She doesn't look up at the sky on her way in to the motel. It's part of the disentanglement; she tells herself on nights like this, "What I did wasn't the end of the world." The sky and the streets and the highway and the houses and the farms are all unchanged. The car. The road. The hills, just to name a few things in her immediate sight to bring her back to now. Her mother's cottage on the left, down through the Oak Hills, the town of Stirling ahead at the bottom, the twinkle of lights, peaceful and sleepy.

She's not one to linger in a state. The stars have served her well over the years in her mental bag of tricks. The stars. The red brocade curtain. The thick pane of glass she pulls down to separate herself from the rest of the world. That, too, is in her head, but is as useful and real as calling the town peaceful and sleepy. For a few minutes, descending the Oak Hills, no longer at the motel in Belleville, not quite home in Stirling, she can let herself believe it.

THEN THERE IS THE small ceramic sun taped above the doorway from the kitchen to the living room. When Celia was a baby, Natha used to walk her around the house pointing out some of her black-and-white framed photographs on the walls. "Flowers. Rocks. Trees," she'd say so Celia would learn the words. "Touch the sun," she'd tell her on their way through the kitchen, holding Celia high so she could tap it.

When she arrives home, Natha touches it herself: this ritual pushes back the sex of the night. It heralds the morning light that is sure to come. She touches it too, to brace herself for what waits in the living room. Devon, spread out on the couch, evidently stoned, his speech slow and slurred.

"That wasn't such a long night," he says.

She believed he'd be in bed right up until she turned onto Edward Street, then she saw the light on in the living room. She believed he'd be in bed because she wanted him not to be in the living room when she got home.

She sits on the loveseat opposite him, already tired of what's ahead.

"I've had longer sessions," she says.

"So ..." he says.

"So," she repeats.

"What's a glassblower like?" he asks, straightening up.

"Did Celia wake up at all?"

"Always the mother first," Devon says with annoyance. "Give me the details."

"Not tonight," she says.

"Not ever anymore?"

"Nothing that hasn't happened a million times before," she lies, deciding the part about her coming would only lead to something she's not up for. She remains a little pissed about that. It's not supposed to happen.

Devon gets up and sits down beside her, stroking her hair.

"It's still wet," he says, leaning in to kiss her neck. "You know I just like to know," he whispers.

"Why don't you just read some Anaïs Nin." She barely points to the coffee table. "Same thing, only she describes it better," she says. But Devon has never had an interest in her books. In any books.

"C'mon," he says, rubbing her neck. "It feeds the marriage." His voice trails off as she leaves the room and heads upstairs.

Natha looks into Celia's room. She sees her sweet, sleeping face, the light from the moon making her golden and prized. Deep in sleep, she isn't aware that Natha kisses her on both cheeks, then her chin, then her forehead, in that order, covering all ground to encase her in her mother's love. This moment puts her night's work behind her. Love can enter now. Natha tiptoes across the hall into her own room and sheds the costume. Tight, dark jeans and a flattering, crisp, white blouse.

It's useless, she concludes, to expect that Devon will ever give up waiting to know the details of her encounters. But what is there to say about the sex? All these years and she still hasn't found the words to say it as it has never been said before. If she can't be original about it, what's the point? Maybe that is the point. Not to try. That would be real. That would be the point.

Christ.

She'll make her pillow damp with her hair.

It smells strongly of the motel shampoo.

Sleep now.

But of course, he comes.

Why should Wednesday, June fourth, be different from any other day?

"What's his story, anyway?" Devon asks, crawling into bed beside her.

"The usual," she answers, rolling over.

"Married. Kids, probably. Just filling a need."

"Something like that."

"Speaking of need," he says, rolling her over to face him.

She doesn't begrudge him the sex she cannot feel, his familiar, boyish need to reclaim her after a night out. He's like a cat pissing around its territory, even though he strays himself. Part of their agreement. Part of feeding the marriage. And isn't the woman of the week named Barb? Or is it Brenda?

She is there and not there and can hardly stand the clicking sound of him lapping around inside her with his mouth, coming up to penetrate her and breathe all over her face.

At least he didn't mention the sisterly thing. When weeks have passed, and she has pushed him away one too many times, he packs it handy, like a gun, reminding her of the reason her father left her mother.

But still, she anticipates it.

And thinks about it while Devon falls asleep.

On nights like this, when she can't sleep, she grabs the flashlight out of her purse and heads for the cemetery at the end of the street. She tries not to veer too far from the here and now. These graves remind her not to. Tonight, there's hardly a need for the flashlight. The moon is full and she thinks it's glad she's here. She didn't notice the full moon earlier, coming out of the motel. It often eludes her, as if she's not meant to find illumination. But tonight it's casting a very bright light, making the headstones of the dead stand out boldly.

They give her permission, the dead. Whatever they did or didn't do in their lives add up to one loud cheer for her to do what it is she does.

They're on her side.

Walking through the cemetery, she wonders what they'd have to say about themselves.

What would she say?

Right now, she would say she's not a stupid woman who spreads her legs for a pittance. She makes money enough and in the spare moments of her life she studies literature in the musty pages of borrowed books from the library. She's photographed the inkling of a bud on a willow bending in the wind, and heard its eight-string song in the acoustics of her head. She is there, and not there, through the paradox of her nights and her days.

She can say that in the dirty little reel some see as the axis of her life she has witnessed beauty like the red-puff face of her newborn Celia and the way the morning light dances lacy yellow on the living room wall. She is rural middle-class; she doesn't wear silk and leather. She wears jeans and flattering, crisp white blouses that hold her teasing breasts. Her eye makeup becomes her calling card and she is not afraid to look into the eyes of a man across the bar, to tell him what she is there for, that she is the one he is supposed to meet tonight. When the dark hotel-room sex is over and she returns home, she plants hair-soft kisses on the cheek of her beloved daughter and then lies down beside her husband and swallows the satisfaction that the sex wasn't so bad and the money good. Some nights she tosses and turns with the queasy scent of something dead, haunted by the memory of the sweat-soaked sheets at the Sunrise; on nights like these, she is in danger of drowning in the confines of the life she cannot altogether give up. She lies uncomfortable, uncertain as to which role is closer to the truth of who she really is.

The man she is married to doesn't want her to give up either role.

Will that be the end of her story? she ponders, gazing at the tall, lichen-covered marble and stone marking these deathly plots of land. She steps accidently on the small, quiet slates lying flat, bearing only the words *FATHER* and *MOTHER*. Farther up the hill there are odd broken headstones, some that have tilted or sunk, while others look like giant chess pieces — a rook, a queen, a king. One, with a carved little lamb on top, for a baby who only lived a few weeks; how did the mother survive the death of her child?

She's made it to thirty-five and Celia to six. She won't consider the possibility that Celia will not outlive her. She heads home, back along Edward Street to her crooked house, which looks like a speck from the top of Oak Hills; a speck in a peaceful, sleepy-looking town where there lives a mother, a father, and their child.

TWO

THE CROOKED HOUSE ON Edward Street is filled with antiques from auction sales — tables from the early 1900s, washstands and wardrobes, and a cherry-coloured Arborite kitchen table from the 1950s; in the hall there are bevelled mirrors and two mahogany bookcases for the books she actually buys. When she and Devon moved in twelve years ago, Natha pulled up the ugly brown shag carpeting and sanded the oak floors herself. Devon watched, helping only to stain the sanded floors. She stripped layers of wallpaper from a few rooms until she got down to the lath and plaster.

She wasn't afraid to get her hands dirty. Still isn't.

She spackled in the cracks in the plaster and painted the rooms with a soft eggshell latex. She added colour to the walls with old paintings and her own photographs of Celia.

Today, she is headed to another auction sale — a John Gulliver sale. "The Clown," she calls him. To Ruthie anyway. And he is a clown, the way he entertains the crowd with his rustic humour. An attractive enough clown, but a clown nonetheless.

Ruthie sits beside her in the car; she is fussing with her hair in the mirror on the sun visor.

"Oh, bloody hell, love," she complains. "Can't do a damn thing with this."

"You're beautiful," Natha remarks.

"You're a liar, love."

Natha lights a cigarette and drives north on the highway to King's Mill, just minutes into the countryside. The ad in the paper mentioned a rolltop desk. She is anxious to see it, to see if it will fit into Celia's room. She'll make it an early graduation gift from grade one, for Celia has done very well this year. She wants a big-girl desk and Natha wants to reward her. Devon told Natha that such a purchase was indulgent. "Exactly," she responded.

"You spoil her," Ruthie says. With her long, worn jean skirt, white cotton gauze blouse, and the three strands of heavy beads around her neck, Ruthie looks every bit the old hippy Natha accuses her of being. With the windows down all the way, Ruthie's long, curly, grey hair with its blond and red highlights blows wildly.

"This *is* Thursday, isn't it, love?"

"Thursday, June fifth."

"It feels like a Wednesday."

"Trust me, Ruthie. It's Thursday."

"Well, damn," Ruthie says. "I'm sixty-bloody-three!"

"Today? I thought it was the fifteenth."

"No, the fifth. Today. I must treat myself to something at the sale."

"I'm sorry," Natha says. "Happy Birthday. Christ. I feel so bad."

"Bad? Hell," Ruthie jumps in. "I'm spending the day with you. What could be better?"

"I can't believe I mixed the dates up like that."

They turn off the highway and drive along the hardened dirt of King's Mill Road and follow Squire Creek, the spring waters flowing westward, towards the silver roof of the old mill. Stones hit the bottom of the car in an unsteady rhythm Natha remembers hearing yesterday, on the road to her mother's cottage. What a departure, she thinks. Yes, the agitation was there yesterday with Irene, which Devon would say he saw coming before she ever left the house. She travels today in a different mood on a different stone-kicking road. The company of Ruthie eases her way; she's felt this ease in companionship since she first met Ruthie just a few years ago — the day Natha went to the library. She had asked one of the librarians to help her with the computer to see if they could find an audio recording of Sylvia Plath's voice.

"Wasn't it around your birthday that we met?" Natha asks.

"My sixticth. I decided I wanted a youthful friend. I picked you."

"No. I picked you. You were new and not from this town so I could be whoever I wanted to be."

"I sure wasn't betting on my new friend being a hooker."

"You took it well when I told you."

"You mean, when you *finally* told me."

"It was the mutual disappointment in hearing Plath's voice that did it," Natha says.

"You were shocked."

"She sounded so old and grave. In my imagination I always heard her voice as sweet and salty in my head."

Sweet and salty, and youthful, Natha remembers. Now it is difficult to read Plath's poems and journals and hear the voice arising from the print as the sweet and salty and youthful one in her memory; in its place, Natha finds the grave, old-sounding tone of Plath's real voice disrupting and disturbing. She wishes she had never heard it. She remembers delving into Sylvia's work when she could, those days cleaning Jules Moore's house. She remembers Plath's life in fully felt details, not as she remembers her own — being initiated into the adult world of sex when she was fifteen and Jules was fifty. "At least Jules was good for something," Ruthie has said, referring to his grand personal library.

On their way to the auction at King's Mill, Natha doesn't bring up her memories or Ruthie's response to when she was told the story. She's not so sure she feels the same way as Ruthie — that the great literature she had her at disposal made up for what it was like lying under the old man.

"Look at that beautiful forest over there." Ruthie is as excited as a child. "It's fully green again. Winter is completely banished."

And that's it — that's what makes Ruthie so different from Irene. Ruthie can be the same age as her mother and still be excited about something as simple as a beautiful day. Irene's happiness is tied up in the first beer, the first Caesar, the drinks that keep her company as she sits on her chair by the water, where she'll have fifteen more. Natha has seen Irene go from irritating sleepiness to happy wakefulness with the pouring of beer or vodka into the morning mug.

"It is lush," Natha says. "So many trees in one clump."

"You can do something for me — for my birthday, love."

"Whatever you want," Natha says.

"Take photos of me naked there, later today."

"You're crazy, Ruthie."

"Crazy? Old and bold."

"Seriously? You want to be photographed in the nude?"

"It's part of reconciling with my body." Ruthie says. "It's something I need to do." Ruthie lost both breasts to cancer at fifty-eight. She has said that she felt her body turned on her. Maybe her husband Edwin's death had brought it on. After the mastectomies and the recovery, Ruthie decided to leave Toronto. She moved to Stirling, where she walks around town without a prosthetic bra and works in the library three days a week. She says she enjoys her slower-paced life. "To hell with money and the smog and the noise."

"How about at sunset?" Natha suggests. "When we're less likely to be seen and the light will be as dramatic as you are."

"Oh, what a glorious idea!" Ruthie claps her hands cheerfully. Natha parks the car near the mill, halfway into the ditch, following suit with the cars ahead of her.

Yesterday's conversation with Devon and last night's slip with the glassblower — she hates to lose control — all of it washes away as she and Ruthie walk across the small bridge over Squire Creek. It comes rushing down from the same direction as the large wetland not so far off to the east, where red-winged blackbirds flit about or stand precariously on the tips of growing bulrushes, leaning in to the shift of the morning wind. It comes spilling over an unspectacular waterfall, over a dam only a few feet high. On the other side of King's Mill Bridge, it slows and swirls and winds its way behind a thicket of ash, maple, and elms until it all but disappears into the woods.

Natha has stood at this exact spot before, in the middle of the bridge, near the aging wall of the limestone mill. She has waited to see if the rush and the trickle from both sides would converge and rise up into nothingness. She pauses now, hoping her mind will be still momentarily without the motel images. She longs to hear nothing, to think nothing.

Once, a number of years ago, she had been inside the old mill. She had driven out to it to sit near the creek. She was there to read one of the books she had borrowed from the library. Her reading was interrupted when a Conservation Authority truck pulled up in the driveway. The mill, the house, and the property surrounding them had been designated heritage properties. There were two people in the truck, a man and a woman. They got out, walked over to the mill, and unlocked the doors and went inside. Natha was sitting across the creek at a picnic table. It was summertime and the creek was low, almost dried up. She decided she wanted to see inside so she closed her book, left it on the picnic table, and walked over to the mill and knocked on the door.

"It's a bit messy in here," the woman said. "With pests coming in from the cold winter. Watch your step."

Natha walked through the raccoon shit and dead bats to find death hanging from a second-floor beam, a shadow swaying against the day's light, swaying in a yellowish tone against the wooden wall. At least that's what she envisioned having heard over the years about Jack Callaberry's suicide — the auctioneer who taught John Gulliver everything he knows. Rumour was Jack was in love with a woman who lived in the schoolhouse down the road, who was married, as he was, and she wouldn't leave her husband and child to be with him. John Gulliver had married Jack Callaberry's daughter, Mary.

The second floor was the darkest of all three in the mill, moody and reeking of the past, history still damp and present in the walls, in the thick beams. It seemed to lie under Natha's feet, carpeting the hardwood floor. She felt its presence behind her no matter what direction she faced. Stone walls don't bleed, they don't die.

She has heard the stories over the years. About the farmers who made their way to the crossroads at Wellman's Corners to the mill to have their logs sawed, their grain ground.

About Rusty Cooter, who got drunk one night and hit his head on the old dam, which still stands half there, several feet upriver from the new one.

About Claudia McMillian, who still lives down the road, who apparently lost her virginity in the summer of '57 to a handful of teenaged boys; willingly, most people who tell this story claim, throwing in the other name for the place — Cherry Mill, which they say with measured amounts of disgust and nosiness in poor Claudia's misfortune. In retelling the story, they never call it rape.

From where Natha stands on the bridge today, with Ruthie looking over the rail at the rushing water, she can't see any of the one-room schools in the area, or the churches or

Wellman's Cemetery, but she knows where they are, up and around the corner, or farther down the road. She sees only the mill and the steel and cement bridge. She hears the sound of the auction crowd gathering up ahead.

She sees John Gulliver, a muscular man of average height, deeply tanned. He stands beside the man who barbeques bratwurst at nine-thirty in the morning. John greets people as they walk onto the grounds, tipping his straw hat, which hides his thick, brown hair and grey-green eyes. He stands with his arms across his chest looking rather subdued. Though they have never really spoken, he always acknowledges Natha's presence with the same nod he gives to everyone. "Dark Eyes," he calls her. "Sold to Dark Eyes for a hundred and fifty."

She likes that he doesn't pay *particular* attention to her. She steels herself for the onset of a large crowd; her back stiffens and the ease of driving here with Ruthie dissipates, a certain toughness taking its place. She doesn't give a shit that she comes across as anti-social or stuck up. Some might say it's reverse snobbery. She walks into the gathering of dealers and collectors and the general public, all of whom have come to buy the items of the dead.

Jarred Forestall, the ad read. *Estate sale.*

It's the smell of a sale she loves. The bratwurst and the old must of old books and old furniture, the cigars and pipes of retired farmers out for something to do. She's been out to John Gulliver's sales many times over the years, acquiring her antique treasures, a long-held dream from the days she used to go out to Jack Callaberry's sales with Daddy. He never bought antiques, just used appliances and a cap for his truck.

Natha would linger by old radios and ornate tables and gold-rimmed dishes, thinking you had to be rich to have them, that people of money furnished their homes with antiques, or had family possessions, the luxuries of the past.

Mostly, she is intrigued by them — these things of history — and she feels the lives of those who sat on the chairs, ate from the plates, bedded down at night on the sheets.

She ponders the secret life of objects.

If only the same people didn't come out to the sales. It's the exchange of glances from recognizable schoolmates and other townspeople she finds hard to take. She has suspected the town's eyes were on her from the time Jules started having sex with her. Jules swore never to tell and of course he didn't; he knew the trouble he'd get in if he did, having sex with a minor *and* paying for it.

Christ, at least *he* isn't here, she thinks, as she walks with Ruthie towards the furniture and scouts out the rolltop desk for Celia.

"Do you mind, Natha, if I head to the tables? I've always wanted to collect Blue Willow, like my grandmother did, and today, well, it *is* my birthday."

"Go ahead," Natha says. "I'll catch up," turning her attention to the desk, opening and closing the rolltop, running her hand along the top, opening a drawer and smelling the scent of its deeply ingrained history. She can feel the hand of a woman writing letters, a woman from the 1930s, she intuits, or imagines — the picture in her mind is more felt than thought out.

"See something you like?"

It's John Gulliver, standing there, behind her, with his straw hat tilted down, his eyes half in shadow.

"The desk," she answers, pointing to it. "What time do you anticipate getting to it?"

He lifts his hat enough so she can see his eyes, and he meets hers head on. She swears to herself, *Don't fucking seek me out like this,* and shifts her own eyes in the direction of the crowd.

"Could be a while. I've got to get through the tables first. You know how it goes."

"Sure," she says.

"Haven't seen you out this year yet," he continues. "Did you ever find a medicine cabinet?"

"You remember that?"

"You wouldn't go over a hundred."

"You remember that too?"

"Last fall. Gary Chalmers' sale on Ridge Road."

Is he looking for points for his great memory? She says nothing, barely smiles. It's one way to respond, to make no move, put a little awkwardness into the air between them. It annoys her that he paid that much attention, that he remembered it. That he stands here now, showing it off.

"I've got another one coming up in a sale next week," he says.

"Another medicine cabinet?"

"A real treasure. Needs a little work, though."

He stands waiting for some kind of response, the clowny grin he regularly wears is not there. He kicks at the ground and looks back up at her with serious eyes, like he has something important to say, something that doesn't have anything to do with a medicine cabinet.

"When?" she asks.

"Tuesday, near the old Harold Cheese Factory."

He glances at his watch.

"Showtime?" she asks.

"A few more minutes," he says and makes no move to leave her. "Natha Cole, right?" He pronounces it correctly. Natha — Nathan without the last "n."

"So, you know my name," she says.

"It's part of my business to know."

So what, she wants to say. Who cares?

"I also know I can never get you to laugh at my jokes."

"Well, don't take it personally. I just don't laugh."

"Never?"

"Rarely. I smile, but I don't really laugh."

"I don't think I've even seen you smile," he pushes on. "You must be the serious sort."

His voice is friendly and his smile seems sincere. Still, she wonders, *Why this, all of a sudden?* She could be jocular about it, she thinks, tell him he's just not that funny, but sometimes he is. He may be sincere and subdued now, but it'll be a different story when he gets on his wooden auctioneer's block, like a windup toy, cranked to sell and entertain, with his small, quick gestures and his rather attractive mouth moving with speed and skill.

"I need to meet up with my friend," she says, looking away from him towards the tables set up in a large implement shed.

She notices the sky is darkening to the west and watches as John heads to his truck and grabs a yellow rain jacket. As she approaches the long tables of glassware and china, she hears Ruthie cooing over the items. She wishes they'd brought umbrellas, not that rain ever dampens her day. She, in fact, loves the rain, the darkness, the moodiness.

"Try not to show such excitement," she advises Ruthie quietly. "See these other people? They conceal their interest because interest always ups the ante."

"Oh, love, what do I know about the goings-on of an auction sale? I've only been to two in my life. But look at this cream and sugar!"

SEVERAL WOMEN ARE GATHERED at one table, picking up and inspecting cups and saucers. They're at every auction, Natha remembers, acquiring more and more. They are almost smug in their simple pleasure — to walk around chewing on phallic pieces of bratwurst, discussing the weather and what the jam cupboard might go for. Natha remains unnoticed by their disinterested eyes. She doesn't consider herself one of them, part of the crowd. She stands back a little, letting Ruthie move farther down the table. She could swear half the town of Stirling is here, the young and the old. And then she spots Sherry Watson from high school — grade ten — walking with an older woman, maybe her mother. Sherry who used to chew fruity candies and used the plastic pencils with tips you could replace. They sat together in the library working on homework during their spare period. Sherry didn't do much work and Natha pretended to, to satisfy the librarian, mostly rewriting previous notes in her good handwriting, nothing that required concentration.

Over that year, Sherry let out tidbits of information. Her

father had committed suicide when she was ten, her mother worked in a factory in Trenton. Sherry was an only child who had to do all the housework. As Natha rewrote her notes, Sherry would drop little bombs. There was a lot of blood. He shot himself. Her mother was sleeping with another married man. She heard them one night. Natha could smell the lead in the pencils and Sherry's strawberry breath. She didn't know why they started sitting together. "It must be hard," was all Natha ever said. It didn't seem that Sherry wanted anything more from her but to be able to sit with someone to pass the time. When she disappeared, Natha felt a twinge of an ache for her — an ache she didn't feel for herself when Irene made her quit school to clean houses and she too just disappeared.

If she learned anything from Sherry and their time in their spare period, it was that most people will hang around for the full story, if given the chance. It's what made Natha sit with her.

As the sale starts, Sherry and her possible mother edge their way into one corner of the shed and John on his box tells the short story of Jarred Forestall's life on this small farm at King's Mill; how he had put up a good fight with the cancer. She hears raindrops falling on the steel roof of the shed and she thinks she could have been a little nicer to this John Gulliver — this fast-on-his-feet farmer boy. And then he begins his strange, melodic chant, which lulls her like music. How absurd, she thinks, to be moved by cadence when what he is doing is selling crocks and moustache cups and Jack-in-the-Pulpit vases. She leans back against the wall of the shed and the head of a nail pokes her. She watches John on his box at the other end of the rippled tin structure, his voice echoing off its rigid, silver walls as he searches the crowd for takers. He flirts with the women before him, no matter what their age, drawing them in.

"Hey, look, I've always been a small man," he says.

"You're not small," one of them shouts.

"I'm not talking about my height or my weight," he jokes.

Laughter, laughter and briefly, swiftly, his eyes keep coming back to meet Natha's, as if he wants to say something. She lets this go on for a while, then she walks outside to have a cigarette, the rain more like mist now. She may feel the secret life of objects, and she has heard and knows the secret lives of many men, but she wonders what it is that John Gulliver would have to say to her. She only knows he's a dairy farmer and that he's married to Mary Callaberry, who she can see now, sitting dutifully on the porch, collecting the money. She too doesn't smile. She is all business.

Natha imagines she makes love the same way, without much feeling.

It's stopped raining. Walking around the property, Natha passes a group of men huddled around a large tractor. She recognizes one of them — Buddy Francis, his blond hair turning white and the hulk of him unchanged by the years. He was one of Daddy's old friends. He looks her way, waves. She walks on, a feeling of repulsion at the sight of him; always this feeling of repulsion whenever she sees him around town, sitting on the bench outside the feed mill, in the post office, the liquor store. As she walks, she remembers how he used to get Daddy going with the booze. Never without a case or a bottle, he was the worst of Daddy's friends. Was there something else? she wonders. Do they share the secret of her father's disappearance? Buddy always bringing up the fact he still hasn't heard from Ray Cole, has she? How many years has it been now, Natha? She walks without responding to his wave, knowing he knows she can't stand him. She's made best efforts when he's within a hundred feet of her or on the very odd occasion he's cornered her. Her repulsion oozes out of her pores as she manoeuvres to get away from him.

She heads back to the shed but, before she can get there, John is coming outside carrying a cane like a shepherd's staff. The crowd follows him outside, out of the shed and up to a line of washstands, flat-to-the-walls, tables and chairs. The rolltop she wants is in this group. John's clerk, a mouse of a man, follows with the auctioneer's box.

"Cole," was all she said when John asked for a name when she won a bid. She wonders who told him her full name. It strikes her it could have been Buddy Francis.

Ruthie appears by her side with the Blue Willow cream-and-sugar set.

"Oh, I am having a good day."

Instead of starting at the beginning of the furniture lineup, John makes his way to the rolltop.

"I thought I'd shake things up a little, keep you folks on your toes by starting in the middle of this fine furniture. Got a lady here who doesn't want to wait. And I may not know a lot, but I know better than to keep a woman waiting for something she has her heart set on."

Ruthie nudges her.

"He's talking about you, isn't he?"

"He's something else," Natha says.

Ruthie nudges her again.

"You've got a way with men, haven't you?"

John starts the bidding on the rolltop. Natha scopes the other bidders. There are only two — a rather hip-looking man in his thirties, and a long-haired picker she's seen at other sales and has talked to briefly. He buys for antique stores in Toronto. It's him she's worried about; playing with someone else's money, he's bound to go higher. And higher he does go. She swears to herself, *Fuck, I want this*, and doesn't bow out; she didn't fuck two guys last week for nothing. *Think of Celia*, she tells herself with every raise of her hand. Devon said it was indulgent but he has no idea. She thinks, *Thank God for the Come What May Account*. And yes, she sees it's over now, the long-haired picker has dropped out —

"Sold, to Natha Cole with the dark eyes."

She smiles, just to give him that, and he winks at her before walking back to the front of the lineup of furniture, only to start again. She walks towards the porch to pay his wife and arrange for delivery of the desk by the same guys who come to every auction with a truck. Buddy Francis, still standing near the tractor, follows her with his eyes; she doesn't have to look to know, she can feel them on her. Sherry shouts her name, waves, and Natha guesses she wouldn't have known it was her if John Gulliver hadn't said her full name. Then again, she thinks, she recognized Sherry, why wouldn't Sherry recognize her? Why wouldn't everyone here recognize her?

"Fuck, don't seek me out," she says under her breath as she hands it over — the cash she's made from other men with secrets of their own.

THEY HOP THE SPLIT-RAIL fence just as the sun is easing its way along the horizon, deep yellows and orange spreading across the end of the day.

"It was a good day, love, you getting that desk, and me with my Blue Willow. It's Flow Blue, some kind woman told me, and it's marked."

"So, it's old and authentic."

"Like me," Ruthie says.

They laugh.

"Devon nearly died when the guys delivered the desk and he saw how old it is, how good it is. 'What the fuck did you pay for this?' he shouted. I ignored him, like I usually do."

"Pretty special that John Gulliver went right to it, just to keep you from waiting."

"That was a little odd."

"That's one word for it." They walk through a field sharing swigs of a bottle of rye and pick a spot in the forest where it isn't too crowded with trees. Natha sets up her tripod, swatting black flies, taking in the smell of the trees, moistened by the day's afternoon mist. It rained hard in the afternoon and she fetched Celia from school with a large umbrella. She experienced enough anticipation to flood the streets of Stirling, hoping Celia would be as excited about her new desk as she was. Devon had reminded her repeatedly that she had to say it was a gift from both of them. *Right*, she thought,

you paid for it. Then she caught herself. He doesn't know about
her Come What May Account.

Somehow, Celia knew where it came from.

"I love you Mommy," she said when she saw the desk set
up in her room. "I love you all the way up to the moon and all
the way to The Chocolate Shoppe and all the way to Foodland
and all the way back home."

Devon stood in the corner of the room waiting for the
thanks that didn't come for several minutes. When it did, it
was like an afterthought.

"You too, Daddy."

Natha could have let herself feel for him at that moment —
he must have felt left out — but she remained outside of it,
experiencing a layer of skin that prevented compassion from
breathing properly through her pores. It's the experience she
has when Ruthie says John Gulliver's wife is a sourpuss. Natha
thinks immediately of the fact that Mary's father Jack Callaberry committed suicide over the jilted love of another woman.
Wouldn't that make a person closed off? The layer of other
skin prevents her from feeling this. The thinking of it comes
easily. The feeling part seems distant and unattainable.

"I suppose that is the likely explanation, Natha. Losing her
father that way."

Ruthie strips off her clothes, piles them neatly on the forest
floor.

"You don't think anyone can see us, do you, love?"

"No. I'd say we're safe." Ruthie stands with her small round
belly and what were her breasts looking like two large staples,
a silvery, purplish colour.

"You're beautiful, Ruthie."

"I'm a little war-torn," she says wearily.

"I'm going to walk back a little Ruthie and do the thirds thing. You know, two thirds of the picture will be the trees on the left, and you'll be standing in the right third of frame."

"Like I'm just another tree?"

"Exactly."

Ruthie straightens, smiles, and then doesn't smile.

"You know, love, it feels kind of good to be here, naked." Ruthie pauses a moment then adds, "Natural."

Natha lines her up in the frame and shoots.

"Will you do me in thirds?" Ruthie asks. "My head and shoulders, then my chest down to my vagina. Then my legs and feet. I can frame them and line them up and down my bedroom wall. Not that I did anything special with my vagina. I didn't give birth with it or anything, like you did with yours."

"I've never asked, Ruthie. Why didn't you have children?"

"We were too much of a couple. Didn't want anything to take away from that."

"I can't imagine that."

"It makes it harder when one of you goes," Ruthie says, pulling a leaf off an elm tree, smelling it.

"I'm going to develop these pictures and frame them," Natha insists. "For your birthday present."

"You're a real dear. You know, I think I'll rub a little dirt on myself too. What do you think of that?"

"Like you're a dirty old girl?" Natha jokes.

"Like I'm of the earth," Ruthie corrects her.

Natha steps back from the camera and watches Ruthie

brush leaves and needles away from the ground and scrape for some soil. Who knows what will happen to her own body over the coming years? So far, good sense and good luck have kept her flesh from harm. But for how long? There must be a God, she thinks, seeing Ruthie spread dirt across her chest. A God that has brought Ruthie to this point in her life, five years later, naked in a forest near King's Mill. A convenient God, she decides, one who keeps Celia safe and healthy no matter what Natha does. A lenient God.

"You should try this, love. It feels so good on the body."

"The only time I've really ever felt good in body was when I was pregnant with Celia, and afterwards, nursing her."

"That's a shame."

"Well, I do have this annoying knot in my back. I do feel that."

Ruthie gives her a sympathetic look.

"You could quit."

"What? Live a normal life and be poor?"

"You've got a brilliant mind," Ruthie says.

"And I've learned to rely on it."

"I know you have."

There's a certain helplessness in Ruthie's voice and she stands with arms dangling by her side. She picks another leaf off the tree and lets it float to the ground.

"Devon could work more," she says, as if she doesn't have a right to say it but says it anyway for Natha's sake.

"This has worked for us all these years. Now, hurry up, we're losing the light."

"All right," Ruthie says. "Oh look, it's turning pink."

"Terrific," Natha says, for a change in the conversation. "You'll be naked and dirty and pink."

But before she turns back to the camera, the glint from the silver roof of King's Mill catches her eye. There was something about Buddy Francis. Now she remembers walking past him, how she felt awkward in her body, then a shiver, as if she was suddenly cold.

She comes back to the camera to shake it off.

Breastless chest.

Vagina.

Feet.

Yes, she thinks. You can run with one, make money with another, mourn the loss of the other. Everything can be cut off or built up or replaced. It's the mind that separates us, makes one person different from the next. The body is only the carrier, the wheels on which our thoughts travel.

THREE

I N THE LIFTING, LINKING days of early June, Natha wipes the
winter's furnace dust off the living room windows. There
is method and then the simple result of accomplishment, the
lacklustre turned into clear-sighted panes onto the outside
world, now in its joyous bloom. The lilac bushes in the far
corner of the garden, morning glories along the fence — these
from *her* outside world, familiar and trusted.

Does an extraordinary life include cleaning windows? she
wonders.

She cleans the windows and catches a glimpse of Devon
cleaning the outside. He is in his Everything-is-Good mood,
leaving streaks from the squeegee she'll have to point out
to him, same thing every spring. She knows his good mood
is due largely in part to his time with Barb last night. It is
Barb, not Brenda. A woman separated from her husband, who
lives near Springbrook. She is childless and childish, accord-
ing to Devon, but he delights in that, that she has tantrums
when he has to return home. He says she likes to be spanked.

He went to her last night when Natha arrived home after photographing Ruthie in the forest.

So be it, she thinks. That's what they agreed to before they ever got married. Devon's philosophy about marriage — a marriage that works and is forever — is about allowing each other pleasures, as long as the other person knows where the line is drawn, as long as you don't fall in love. Devon believes himself to be a philosopher. So be it, again. At least he is too busy, too happy with himself today to try to insist she is something other than she is. So far, he hasn't tried to tell her she is sad because today is Daddy's birthday. So far, she's hardly thought about it, busying herself with domesticity.

She passes between windows and sees a spot above a wingback chair where she could put a medicine cabinet; it could display the rocks she and Celia collect. Maybe she will go to the next sale. On the table beside the chair are the journals of Sylvia Plath and Anaïs Nin, which she pulled out of the bookcase last night, vowing to reread them; it has been years, and she has been thinking of both women for a while now, wondering if setting down the details of your life makes it seem longer. At least it can be remembered, she thinks, herself still missing chunks of her own life. Even early this morning, when she took Celia down the street to play with her friend Amy, Natha walked back along Edward Street alone, remembering she used to play with Buddy Francis's daughter when they were six. She recalled Darlene's blond, almost white hair flying by her in a flash. She thinks it was in the kitchen, but that was all she remembered. The swoosh of Darlene's hair.

The phone rings, interrupting her thoughts. It's Irene calling to tell her not to be feeling bad because it's that old bastard's birthday. It was the same when Daddy left. Irene would say, *Now, don't you walk around feeling sad about your father. Don't feel miserable. Don't feel angry. Don't feel.*

No wonder the dulling happened, she thinks, when she gets off the phone.

Twenty-one years now since he left. There ought to be a calendar just for that. But no, she thinks, it's the seventh day of June and I'm going to enjoy it with nothing on tonight but a little reading, no lumberjack to shuffle in and out of the Sunrise Motel, no trees to be felled.

She could write now, make a journal entry if she had a journal. Saturday, June seventh. Too hard to be in a bad mood when the lilacs are in bloom and your husband, happy in post-coital bliss with someone else, is cleaning the windows and leaving you alone to be in whatever mood you're in. If only you could decide what mood that is. Not gritty enough, poetic enough, not interesting. Always this search for words, the energy of Plath and Nin, but everything comes out of her in plain, dull language and she has always envied those who could record the words as though their lives depended on doing so. To be so interested in your own life, how is that done?

What could she say about Daddy? His complete disappearance from her life is now like old dust in her soul, not as easy to clean, wipe away. At least she can do something tangible with the windows. The dust inside is stirred up anyway and she gets a rush of feeling, thinking about seeing Sherry yesterday at the sale, still looking the same, just older, Sherry and her mother without the father who shot himself. And Mary Callaberry, John Gulliver's wife, the daughter of Jack Callaberry who hanged himself in King's Mill. Two daughters of two men who killed themselves. She has considered this herself, about Daddy, that maybe he killed himself or got killed and that's why he never came back. Spraying the window, wiping the cleaner away, the thought runs through her, knowing full well it isn't likely, remembering that last image of him, the day he left. She saw him from a window getting into his truck. As he did, the truck bounced. Bouncing for joy for escaping, she thought, watching him drive away. He's probably happy, not dead.

She starts on the last window, catches a glimpse of Devon out of the corner of her eye. It seems fitting to her that Devon be on the outside, in her peripheral vision. Her love for him feels peripheral, she has said as much to Ruthie. It's only Celia she holds closely, dearly, fully.

The phone rings again. Amy Bloom's mother calling to see if Celia can stay for dinner.

"Yes, I think so," Natha says, hesitantly. She wanted to spend the day with her, but Celia wanted to play.

"Actually, Natha, the girls were even talking about a sleepover."

"Not tonight. I don't think Celia's ready for that."

"She seems like she wants to, and I wouldn't mind at all."

Natha hesitates again, feeling uneasy that Celia is now at the age when she chooses a friend over her, over their bedtime ritual of a handbook.

"Some other time, maybe, once I've had the chance to talk to her about it," she says into the phone, not wanting to make Amy's mother feel like there's something wrong, but there is something wrong, Natha thinks, that she's not ready to let Celia go in this way. Not yet.

The sun fades into cloud and shadow spreads across the room and across her heart. Celia will be disappointed.

"Who was that?" Devon asks, walking in, sweat gathered in his curls.

"Amy's mother. Celia's staying for dinner."

He spreads himself out on the couch, sighs as though he's had enough of the cleaning. She doesn't tell him that Celia wants to stay overnight, doesn't want to take the chance he'll talk her into it.

"I'm spent," he declares.

"I suppose you are," Natha says. "Where did you meet this Barb?"

"*This* Barb," he says, mocking her. "At the garage, where else? Came in for tune-up. I told her she needed new shocks."

"Are you going to start on the deck today?"

She wants time alone in the house, to read, to move about without his presence, without his little tidbits about his tryst with Barb thumbtacking her day.

"I think I'll just stay here for a while, rest up. Start later. Or tomorrow. Want to smoke a joint?"

"I'll pass," she says, running through her mind what else she can do if she doesn't want to stay here with him. Once he's stoned he'll want to ruminate their life together, his way of letting her know she's still number one. *The wife. The life.*

"Can you take that outside?" she suggests. She doesn't allow for smoke of any kind in the house.

"She'll be out all day," he whines.

"Please," she says.

"Come out with me. We can talk."

"I've got errands to run," she tells him, thinking it's as good as any day to go to Stedman's for socks and buttons and wool to make puppets with Celia. She'll show it all to her tonight to ease her disappointment about not being allowed to stay at Amy's.

Maybe her love isn't so full. Maybe she needs Celia more than Celia needs her. These puppets are her ploy to make her daughter happy to be at home, instead of at a friend's. Manipulation, she thinks. I am manipulating my daughter's emotions.

She must try not to do this. But the decision is already made and so she'll make the best of it and cuts out on Devon and his dope and his post-coital high in favour of Mr. and Mrs. Sock.

Walking down Edward Street she can't help but realize there's loneliness in loving Celia as much as she does, or maybe she just equates love with loneliness. She loved Daddy, in all his largeness, rough as he was, drunk as he was. Except for that time in her room when he walked in on her. She was dressed only in a bra and underwear. He told her she was filling out nicely. He never made any other comments about her being a girl. He took her fishing, showed her how to change fuses in the fuse box and set up a mousetrap. Things she never saw him do with Jimmy J.

When Daddy left, she hung on to the lonely feeling that permeated her life. To hang on to it meant Daddy was still there, for you only feel lonely if you've loved, and when that got hard, she just replaced it with money, the money she made cleaning houses, then with the money she made by having sex at fifteen with fifty-year-old Jules Moore.

Funny, she thinks, she doesn't feel lonely when Devon isn't around, when he's out having sex with other women, when he goes away fishing up north with his old friend Terry. The thing about Devon is, he's always come back to her, to the marriage.

With Celia now wanting more time with her little friends, Natha feels the loneliness of love again. And the lonely feelings bring back her memory of Daddy. She walks past the Mill Pond and slowly past the feed store, stopping to look inside the window. She sees the same old chairs there where Daddy used to sit shooting the shit with the likes of Buddy Francis. The one chair — a steel frame with cushy, well-worn, red leather and a dip in the bottom where Daddy sat his ass down — there, she thinks, is where he must have thought about leaving, because she never caught him in a faraway trance of thought at home.

At Stedman's Department Store, she is disappointed with the selection of socks. She wants something classic, not black dress socks and white sport socks. She digs through the assortment until she finds grey ones with white toes and heels. Not a hundred percent cotton or wool, but the little bit of polyester she can live with. She scans the store, not remembering where the buttons are, and the wool, and then she spots him, near the kitchenware, examining a spatula, age spots on his hand where the skin is translucent. That hand had rubbed her clitoris until she came, a teenager in his service, under his literary guidance, in the washing of his floors, in his bed.

It was Jules who introduced her to Sylvia Plath and Anaïs Nin, those intense women who sat on his bookshelf and promised escape. He was "Mr. Moore" when she first started cleaning his house, then "Julian" when he sat and chatted about his literary favourites, then "Jules" when he presented it to her one day — the seventy-five dollars and the deal, told her it would be a little uncomfortable the first time, that she should get on the pill. He was clammy and out of breath and it really did hurt as he punctured her hymen and all she wanted to do was pee. Irene was taking all of her money from the cleaning jobs. This, she thought, would be all hers. She was sick of working for nothing, and on it went until he became too dependent and she stopped seeing him once she was old enough to move on to others.

This town is too small, she thinks, and now she is stuck with him in Stedman's, his mind narrowed to the task at hand. When she's seen him from far away, she's managed to avoid him. But it's been a few years, she hasn't seen him. Where has he been?

She still needs to get the wool and the buttons, and so she won't leave. Besides, she is curious to see what he'll do with her sudden appearance. Who did he ever think he was, the once prominent town bookseller, sleeping with a fifteen-year-old and paying for it? The thought of startling him appeals to her.

"Jules," she says from behind him, loud enough to make him jump.

He turns around to face her voice.

"You," he says, surprised. "Natha."

He moves in closer. He's wearing brown trousers and a yellow shirt. His eyes dark and yellowing. His greying black hair has thinned and is limp-looking.

"Well, I'll be damned," he says. "Look at you."

His hands are shaky as he stands there holding the spatula the way a child holds a toy, close to his chest. He used to be tall; he has shrunk and lost weight and his skin is sallow. The surprise, she thinks, is all hers. He's literally like a ghost from her past.

"You look well, Natha. How long has it been?"

She isn't sure if he means the last time they ran into each other, or the last time they spent time together. She initiated this, she thinks, she'd better be civil.

"Well, I've had a child since then and she's six."

"I know, I know, I heard. Living a different life, are you?"

Amid the clothes and the baby pools and sewing instructions, it strikes her as remarkable that the two of them should be standing here, near the kitchenware and the hair colour. It strikes her that he changed the course of her life and now stands before her just a shell of himself. She thinks she could rip him apart with one cutting remark, but she won't. It's poetic justice that he looks so small now.

"You know, I've wanted to talk to you, Natha." His voice is low and secretive and she chooses this as a time to cut out.

"I've got to go," she says loudly. "So good to see you. I'm

getting some supplies and then going home to cook dinner for my daughter," she lies while a few people make their way to the pots and pans. She knows he is one for appearances and counts on it, and he doesn't make a fuss.

"I'll see you around," he says.

Of all places, she thinks. Stedman's. Buying a bloody spatula. And she's aware just now that it isn't called Stedman's anymore, hasn't been for ages, and she realizes that when she walks around town she never really looks up and only knows the stores by the paces in between and by the goods they sell. The only store she knows for sure by name is The Chocolate Shoppe, because Celia talks about it all the time. Stedman's isn't Stedman's anymore, and Jules isn't Jules anymore.

She grabs some red wool for Mr. and Mrs. Sock's hair, and buttons in many colours. She checks out quickly and heads home, passing the feed mill once again and the Mill Pond. She feels like a game piece landing on certain places during a race to the finishing line on a game board where there is no winning. The feed store. The Mill Pond. Home.

SHE WEIGHS TELLING DEVON about running into Jules. They sit outside and smoke a joint together at the picnic table in the back — her first in a long time. She feels the need to do something they used to do in their early years together. Smoke joints, watch movies, share some wine. He doesn't bring Barb up again. She doesn't bring up Jules, or the fact Celia wanted to stay overnight at Amy's, or that she saw Buddy Francis the other day at the auction, or that she plans to go to another John Gulliver sale on Tuesday to check out the medicine cabinet.

She wants it to be just them.

They smoke in silence, sharing only how good the pot is.

"You'll be real happy in a moment," Devon says, handing her the joint. He rubs his nose and opens a wide smile, as if he is handing her the most precious present, a piece of their past.

"Going to go grab the guitar," he says, jumping out of his seat, coughing and hacking on his way into the house.

So this is the way it goes, she thinks. When you can't move forward together, you go back. It's how it started with them. Devon hustling her in a bar fourteen years ago while she was waiting to meet a client, bringing out his guitar and playing it over top of the bar music on the speakers. He was asked to leave. He convinced her he was the one she was supposed to meet that night.

He plays his "Stacks of Gold" song for her and she tries to pay attention to the words, but all she hears is the strumming of the strings.

She's not stoned, not really, and she's hardly had any wine.

Any minute now, she tells herself, she will hear the words, really hear them. They should come back to her, the way Devon comes back to her.

Any minute now, she should feel the effort.

Any minute now.

She should feel.

"I'VE GOT A SURPRISE for you," she tells Celia on their way home from Amy's.

"Why couldn't I have a sleepover?" Celia says, confused.

"I thought we should talk about that first, before you do."

"Why?" Celia asks.

"So you will know what it's going to be like," Natha says, as if she has memories of such a thing herself. She doesn't remember ever staying at a friend's house. She didn't have any friends. That anyone ever talked to her was a surprise when she was growing up, isolated as she was in her need not to be known. She was the one who lived in the crooked house on Edward Street, full as it was with dirty shoes and screaming walls, Daddy and Irene's voices trapped in the kitchen mostly, where all friends would have to pass through.

"Why?" Celia asks again. "What do I need to know?"

"I just think you're still a little young, sweet girl."

"But I'm a big girl!" Celia stomps her words along with her feet.

"I didn't say you can't. I just want to talk about it first. That's all."

"So, next time I can, Mommy?"

"Yes," Natha assures her, vowing to keep her promise and not be sideswiped by the idea.

They pass another mother with a daughter maybe a year or two older than Celia. The woman smiles and says "Hello." Natha returns the gesture. She has seen the woman before, working in the deli section at Foodland. The responsible mother type of woman, she thinks; someone who doesn't sneak out of her child's bed to meet a man at a motel. Someone who works at the same job day in and day out, asking "What will it be today, sir?" They aren't much different, anticipating people's needs, the gestures, what might be said, how to make them happy.

The bank tellers and the grocery store clerks. They all lose a little of themselves by day or night. She wonders, does the deli woman notice their daughters' sandals flip-flop in unison?

I couldn't live your life, Natha imagines saying to this woman; if they were to talk and if she was truthful, and she imagines that this other mother would tell her, *I couldn't live your life either*. And if she knew what Natha does for a living, she'd probably make it harder than it is, or softer with her own images of what sex is, or not hard enough.

Tonight, they are just two mothers. Tomorrow, they'll both be serving someone else. In Natha's mind, this notion casts their lives somewhere between the brilliant yellow light of the early evening and the coming dark shadows of the trees and the houses. They all but disappear at their front doors.

What happened in your day? she'd like to ask.

Something happened today in light of Daddy's birthday and Irene's urging not to feel anything, and Devon's aftermath smile and Jules's sudden appearance and Celia's disappointment that she can't spend a night with a friend. What happens in a day, Natha thinks, that isn't tied like an umbilical cord to the rest of our sensational and sorry lives? She herself, a Virgin/Whore of the Meaning of Day, not seeing it at all, or seeing too much.

She could have stopped the deli woman in the street and told her that something else happens during the dark-room sex at the Sunrise, that there's more to the exchange than flesh, that she feels the truth of the men's lives — their character traits and their memories, their wives, their children, their parents — with every releasing breath. It's when she hears her own breath that she gets scared, proof that she exists outside of her observations. Does it scare you too, to know you exist but haven't a clue who you are? Are you the woman who just put her child to sleep with whispers that dreams come true, or the woman in bed at a motel making a man's dreams come true, or the woman who passes through the red brocade curtain in your mind, passing through one life to the other, always just passing through?

TOMORROW, SUNDAY, JUNE EIGHTH, she'll be sitting at a table in the dark-panelled, upscale restaurant in downtown Belleville, wearing a marigold-coloured sundress for Roberto. He'll know to come to her table. She'll watch him move quickly, gracefully from the kitchen to other tables, his sturdy, stocky body will come right up to her when he returns with a glass of wine and a basket of bread.

She has been through this before with him. He asks her to arrive near the end of the lunch shift, when he gets off. He likes to watch her while he works, to think about what will happen between them later.

"What a beautiful dress," he will say through his dark red lips.

"I don't have many," she will tell him.

They have had this conversation before, about the same dress.

"Summer-sex yellow," he will whisper in her ear.

He will bring two chocolate covered strawberries for dessert.

He will want her to take a drive with him in his van, out to the countryside, where he will make love to her on some road.

He will bring her a cognac to warm up to the idea.

She will sip it, loving the fire in her mouth.

He wants her to be his girlfriend in this scenario and they must make love, not fuck. He likes that she can be impatient with him, rude even. Says it reminds him of his wife, the way she used to be when they were still married. Now she is nice to him. He talks about his wife, his daughter, his mother. She's been wearing black every day since his father died a year ago. Roberto lives with her, gives most of his money to his ex-wife.

"You still love her," Natha will say again as they drive south across the Bay Bridge into Prince Edward County.

"I still care for her," he will admit, like he has before. He will lean over and open the glove box, grab a can of beer, pat his bulging stomach, and say, "I drink too many of these."

The sex will be lethargic, Roberto dragging it out in the back of his van, parked in the grassy laneway of a farmer's field, just off of a county road. He only moves quickly when he is working.

She will be glad to get it over with, to get out of the day's stark light.

She already knows how it will go, writing the script before the film begins.

FOUR

THE DAYLIGHT IS TOO much, it fills the van and she is able to see herself.

Roberto has pushed her dress up to her neck. She keeps catching glimpses of her legs wrapped around him. This sight interferes with the process. He pushes her legs up close to her face and she sees the white, pebble-shaped scar on her kneecap, which she got from falling during a track meet in school, landing on some stones. Daddy said, "It looks like one of them is stuck in there forever." Now it makes for unwelcome awareness of her body.

Fuck, she thinks. *Fuck*.

Roberto is mechanical in his moves, odd for someone who wants to "make love," all of his sensuality tied up in talk, unable to transmit it physically.

Her body is pinned to the floor of the van. The smell of the hayfield blows in from the windows and marries with Roberto's beery breath. She hears the cars out on the paved county road, whizzing by. Closer, she hears the sound of a tractor.

There is too much life around out here and the smell of a hayfield growing is more permeating than the smell of the sex.

The summer Daddy left — before he left — he took her with him to help a farmer friend bring in the first cut of hay on land just north of Stirling, down a road that scissors through tunnels of trees and up and down steep hills. The truck was like a coffin for the dust. Daddy's country music blared from the radio and, in the leathery heat, she hoped she was up for the job, eyeing the rectangular bales in the fields they passed. If she curled up in a fetal position she'd be the same size. Could she pick up the weight of herself, she wondered. Daddy's friend still baled the old-fashioned way with relic equipment making rectangular bales, not the huge round bales she saw when driving by other farms.

The white clapboard house at the farm smelled of bleach and milk and cow manure. There were little kids running around half dressed, screaming and playing. She couldn't wait to get away from them and out into the fields, where she would show Daddy how strong she really was. A few men and a couple of their brawny sons had gathered. Daddy said Jimmy J. was useless, hanging out at Oak Lake, chasing girls. "He's a sissy of a man." But his daughter, by the Jesus, Natha may look like a girl, but she was all boy inside. The men and their sons chuckled. She lifted her first bale onto the wagon, carrying it lengthwise as Daddy had told her. The hay pricked her legs and the bottom of her chin with the stiff cuttings. She nearly passed out from the exertion. The sons just smirked and she wanted to kick them where it counts for disliking the fact she was even there.

She stayed all day, bringing hay in, taking breaks only when the rest of them did until Daddy called for another go-round. Her T-shirt was soaked and her jeans stuck to every inch of her legs, but she got back to work. The brawny boys stared and licked their lips in unison when their eyes levelled at her crotch.

"You'd do best to keep your smart asses moving with a bale," Daddy said when he spotted them. It was like he had put a coat around her shoulders on a freezing mid-winter night.

ROBERTO PULLS OUT SUDDENLY, reaches for his nearby beer, and takes a long swallow.

"I don't feel like you're with me," he sighs.

The nearness of the tractor makes her less than patient.

"From now on, it's the motel," she says sharply.

"Take it easy," he says, taking another swig.

She lies in the van, her mind somewhere between wanting Roberto to finish so she can keep all the money, and wanting to shove him out of her way so she can leave the van and light up a cigarette in the field. Her fourteen-year-old hay-lifting self blew off her watched crotch and pushed herself out beyond the looks of the brawny boys. She took in the smell of the hay and welcomed the day's dirt. It was like she was intruding or trespassing. When Daddy puffed asthmatically, giving into the boulder of his belly, he retreated to the farmer friend's truck for a rest and a few more bottles of beer. He lost his watchful eye and didn't hear the brawny boys whisper, "We want to fuck you." She walked away, *scum* repeating in her head.

She wants to tell someone — Daddy — that the brawny boys in the hayfields called her a dirty girl.

They didn't see her strength, experience the tear of her muscles with every lift of a bale, or feel the itch of her skin from the stiff hay. They didn't see that she carried her own weight. She kept going. She showed up the next day, just to go through it all again, and to say "fuck you" to their faces. That was the first time she stiffened her back against the world.

RUBBING HIS PENIS AGAINST her, Roberto pleads, "I really want to come."

"Then love me," she says, hating that her youthful *fuck you* has turned into a *fuck me and get it over with*.

She only tells them *fuck you* in her head now, while uttering *love me*, like now with Roberto. But in the background of her thoughts, just as vivid as Roberto in the van, is the image of Jules, seventy now, frail with a spatula in his hand. He said he'd been wanting to talk to her. What could he possibly have to say?

She is glad Jules is frail now, looking used up, with his yellow eyes and yellow skin. It diminished him, towering over him in Stedman's like that, even though now they look to be the same height; he has lost inches and that makes him lose some of his old power.

It is much easier to disappear in the dark room of a motel, she thinks; here, in the van, in the middle of the afternoon, she cannot eliminate the reality of what is going on now, the mechanical movements of Roberto. Images of Jules. How did she get from being the fourteen-year-old *fuck you* girl to the compliant fifteen-year-old in Jules's bed? She feels fifteen again, compliant in this van.

The heat of the day alone is exhausting her, never mind her thoughts racing to Daddy, then Jules, now Irene.

Daddy left. Irene made her quit school. Jules promised freedom.

Roberto comes, then falls against her, kissing her neck.

"I could love you," he whispers. She wants to push him off, but *lie here, lie here* she hears in the disappearance of the tractor in the distance and the cars on the road and Roberto's quieting breath.

See, it's not so bad, she says. To whom is she speaking now? The boy in her arms and still between her legs? The girl in her breasts? The dutiful daughter in her hands? Once the man has stopped talking, and stopped touching, and stopped, just stopped, she can anticipate her departure and go home with the money. Go home to her world, even if it is a little world, in a little town where everyone notices everything.

"We should go now," she tells him.

"First, a cigarette," he says, getting up.

She follows him outside, her dress out of shape, her hair knotted. They stand in the hayfield. She tries to fix herself, reset herself.

"Thank you for that," she says. She needs to be nice. Word of mouth and all that. He's a regular. He has sent others to her.

"You're too upscale today to be standing in a hayfield," he laughs.

He puts an arm around her and blows smoke into her face.

"There'll be snow in this field before I can afford to see you again," he jokes.

"From now on," she says, "it's the motel and a pair of jeans. No more fields."

"You don't like the hayfields?"

"Not like this," she says. "And not in a dress."

ALL THOSE YEARS AGO, in the hayfield, when she straightened her back so as to be unaffected by the brawny boys, she pictured a smaller version of herself inside herself, an outline, a tiny figure demeaned and scared, and then she started to breathe; and, in her head, every time she exhaled, the smaller outline of herself grew bigger and bigger until the outline pushed through her real skin into a vast blue light around her and everything the brawny boys said and did bounced off the blue light, tiny sparks that landed on the ground as ashes.

That day, out there in the hayfield with the brawny boys, was the first time she was conscious of pushing herself out. It came to her so easily that over the years she has wondered if it wasn't there before, from even earlier in her life. She just can't remember that time; how old she was, and why. She only feels it is the secret of this ability, but she didn't call on it today in the van. She was distracted, letting herself think of Daddy and Jules; resigning herself now, as she finishes her cigarette, to the possibility there must be a reason she chose not to push herself into the vast blue light outside the van.

FIVE

"ANOTHER FUCKING AUCTION," DEVON says in the kitchen, shaking his head.

She has left it to the last minute to tell him, and has done so only out of necessity, in case she arrives home with an antique medicine cabinet. The rest she keeps to herself — seeing Buddy Francis, running into Jules, the memory of haying with Daddy. Her private running narrative of the past few days. She doesn't want Devon's spin on any of this. Besides, she thinks, part of maturity is keeping most of your life to yourself.

She pours a bowl of cereal for Celia, who is waiting at the table with one sock puppet on her hand. It has two eyes but only a few strands of red wool for the hair.

"Mommy, can we do the rest of the hair on Mrs. Sock tonight?" she asks.

"What the hell are you going to another auction for?" Devon asks, leaning into her.

"Mommy!"

"A medicine cabinet — I want one for the living room.

Here, sweet girl, eat your cereal. And yes, we can do the hair tonight."

"Outside, now," she says to Devon, leading the way from the kitchen into the garage.

"Don't swear like that in front of Celia. You know I don't like it."

"Well, what the fuck is with you?"

"Is that the only word you know, Devon?"

"Did you make that much money the other day with Alberto?"

"You can't even keep the names straight," she says sharply. "His name is Roberto. And don't tell me what to do with the money."

"It's one big pot. At least I thought it was."

"Of course, it is. But you know I can't stand it when you tell me how to spend it. You weren't the one fucking for dollars in a field."

"Look," he says, getting close to her, letting the anger out of his body. "If you want a fucking medicine cabinet, get one. Just don't tell me we don't have any fucking money."

"And just when was the last time I did that?"

"That's not the point, Natha."

"It's exactly the point. The money just magically appears, doesn't it, Devon? All on its own."

"Wow! Where the fuck are you coming from?" He steps back, takes a long drag on his cigarette, and shakes his head, staring at her. "Why don't you go back to bed and get up all over again."

"Fuck you," she says and goes back into the house. She

knows she's made him an easy target for her unsettled sleep last night. She couldn't decide to go to the cemetery and shake it off, so she tossed and turned. Her body was too tired, but her mind wouldn't shut off with what she saw the other day, her knees almost to her face in the van with Roberto. She feels mad, mad as hell this morning that Devon was even there when she got up.

She wanted to be alone. To wake up with the bed and her thoughts to herself, no bodies, she thought, Christ, no more bodies around me. She wanted to wake up after very little sleep and correct and erase the jarring reminders of Daddy and Jules, take the time to get back into the vast blue light. But Devon was there, telling her to get up and go to Celia, he needed to sleep a little longer.

"Hey," he says now, standing in front of the garage, wiping his nose, anxiously, as she's getting into the car to take Celia to school and then off to the auction. "Hey, I love you. Both of you."

He's got the look of a scolded child, his arms hanging limp at his sides, as if he couldn't help it, he just has to throw his weight at her from time to time, to be the man. Has she bruised him? She feels sorry for him, standing there like that, like she's the stronger of the two and isn't supposed to show it. Or is it that she's unable to yield to any man, and so she fights with Devon for questioning the way she spends their money by making it all about how she earns that money when it isn't about the money at all.

IT IS NOT LOST on her that she ends up in yet another hay-field today, this one being used as a makeshift parking lot for the sale. The sharp smell of the hay makes her feel slightly nauseous and she considers leaving, forgetting all about the sale and the medicine cabinet, but she does not want to go home. She walks on to the front lawn of the house, a fieldstone house with deep purple shutters, the kind of house that has been fixed up by someone who loves antiques. She checks her watch. Nine a.m., an hour before the sale. Tuesday, June tenth, she reminds herself. In a pissy mood, she thinks, eyeing a dark patch in the sky she didn't see on her way out. It twirls into itself, then spreads out and moves towards her. The sky darkens and the light begins to look like that of late afternoon in October. The trees beginning to sway frantically. Without an umbrella or raincoat, she has no choice but to turn around and head back to her car to wait out the storm.

Huge fat drops land on the windshield. She opens her window only slightly, enough to let the air in and let out the smoke from her cigarette. She can't remember the last time she was caught in a storm, but the sky's striking moodiness suits her. Teeming, like her memories, as much sensations as specific events. Sunday in the van, remembering how that first *fuck you* to the boys felt. Strong and alive, like she would steer her own ship in life.

And now bewilderment falls like the sheets of rain. She is back in her room — the one that was hers growing up — looking out the window as the rest of the summer that Daddy left passes by and the rains come but no phone call or letter, not a word of any kind. It was like she'd been cut in two. She moved through her days an amputee, a talking, walking stump, always tripping over reminders. His faded blue corduroy

La-Z-Boy chair, old workboots covered in the white paint he used to paint the garage that spring, empty mickey bottles of rye she'd find in the oddest places.

Not just her own life changed in that first year Daddy was gone. Irene worked the early shift at Ren's, waitressing, and drank from the time she got home until she passed out, barely making dinner anymore. Natha hit her schoolbooks with a thirst for something else to think about. Jimmy J., older and just as messed up, took to drugs and break-and-enters; he had already quit school.

She's always blamed her diligence with her schoolwork for giving Irene the idea that Natha was capable of working to help pay the mortgage. She had the discipline, Irene told her, to run her own business, cleaning houses. Grade ten ended and Natha didn't go back for grade eleven. She went, instead, into the houses of the town's old ladies and the well-off, the kind of people who could pay her regularly to clean their luxurious lives up. That's how she thought of it, cleaning people's little lives up. She couldn't stand their exhaustive lists of chores — the neatness and order of their lives — while hers grew dirtier all the time, the house on Edward Street imploding with booze and drugs and very little food to eat. She knew she would have been better off living alone. She could hardly take Jimmy J.'s smartass mouth or Irene's love affair with the beggar juice. That's what Natha came to call the booze — beggar juice— watching Irene beg for relief from anxiety and loneliness. In Jules's house, filled with books, she could immerse herself in other, more interesting lives. He wasn't that picky about how she cleaned his house and would often leave books out for her to read. She'd stay an extra hour to find out what it was like for Sylvia Plath to start catching a poem, and for Anaïs Nin, who was angry she couldn't find a publisher to publish her work so she bought her own press and published her own books. That's what *she* did with her anger; she turned it into action.

No wonder she saw Jules's proposition as a way to rule her own life. No one else was going to be concerned about it. No one else even asked.

THE BEWILDERMENT OF THE sudden rain is in line with her bewilderment that this is where she has ended up, with Sunday's paying sex still muscling in on the indiscriminate centre between her legs, buying antiques for a house she's never been able to leave.

The bewilderment dances with a kind of loneliness she hasn't felt for a long time. She rolls her window down a little more. It's June, she thinks, Tuesday, June tenth, in a whole other time.

She's a wife now.

A mother.

She calls the shots of with whom, when, where, and how.

She closes her eyes to all the women she has come to be.

When she opens them, John Gulliver is standing alongside her car, just outside her window, with a large black umbrella, grinning with amusement, like he's been standing there watching her without her knowing.

She rolls the window down all the way.

"What are you doing?" she asks, her voice rising in surprise.

"I'm here to escort you to the sale," he says, opening the door. She hesitates, puts her cigarette out in the ashtray.

"I'll wait until it stops," she says.

"C'mon," he urges. "It's only water."

"Do you do this for everyone?" she asks, getting under the umbrella with him.

"I saw you pull in, then walk onto the lawn, then disappear. I can't have you disappearing before the sale even starts."

"I may not stick around," she says.

"Just stay close to me. The medicine cabinet is over here."

He seems nervous and excited; does he have something invested in this? He looks at her so seriously, a crease in his brow, a straight mouth.

"I was hoping you'd come," he says, leading her back towards the house, onto the lawn, past a string of antique side tables and bookshelves, an antique telephone bench and a blanket box, a row of antique chairs, until they come to the medicine cabinet, painted white with chips in the paint and a mirror where the silver backing has come away in the corners. It has carved scrolls down the sides and a wooden cross carved within a circle at the top.

"I've never seen one like it," he says. "They got it somewhere in the Eastern Townships of Quebec. It's either something religious or something to do with the Red Cross. They don't remember the exact story. No one remembers the stories anymore."

She crouches down to get a better look, opens it up, and inspects the shelves, which are in good shape.

"It's definitely old," she says.

"Like I said last week, it needs a little work. Strip it, clean it up."

"No," she says. "I wouldn't change a thing. I love it the way it is."

"Seriously? You'd leave it like this?"

"Seriously," she answers. "It has character." She stands up. "Don't we do enough of that? Love something for what it is, then change it?"

"Are we talking about antiques, or what?"

"Yes," she says. "What else?"

"Like I said, I've never seen one like this. I expect a lot of interest."

"Just keep your eye on me, John Gulliver."

"I intend to."

The crowd begins to move farther along the tables set up on one side of the lawn. Others inspect the furniture and the medicine cabinet.

"What do you think it'll go for?" she asks him.

"I have no idea. Something like this could go for any amount."

"Oh, come on. You've been at this a long time."

"Over thirty years," he says.

"I remember when you worked with Jack Callaberry."

"You remember that?"

"Yes."

"He taught me everything I know."

"Too bad what happened to him."

"People don't know the half of it," he says, looking past her now. "I'll be right back. Here. Hold the umbrella." He leaves her side to talk to his wife, who is standing on the porch, visibly impatient, waiting for him.

Natha watches John almost run to her and she doesn't know if it's the rain making him run or the look on Mary Callaberry's face. She sees him talking to her now, his arms gesturing in argument. Definitely not the rain, she thinks, moving over a bit so some couple can take a look at the cabinet. She eavesdrops on their conversation, and is relieved when they decide they want something simpler for their bathroom.

A young girl with blond hair rushes by almost bumping into her. The rush of the fair hair leaves Natha feeling off-balance, almost faint, and she takes a deep breath, which she exhales with an unexpected feeling of panic. She sees another rush of young blond hair in her mind — Darlene, Buddy Francis's daughter.

"Sorry," John says when he returns. "My wife wanted to talk to me."

"Everything okay?" Natha asks, not really wanting to know because she suspects Mary's impatience has something to do with him standing here under the same umbrella as her.

"Sure," he says. "For the most part."

In his presence, the flash of Darlene's blond hair disappears from her thoughts.

"You said people don't know the half of it about Jack Callaberry."

"They don't. And I've never talked about it. Not even with her," he says, nodding in the direction of his wife, still standing on the porch.

Natha decides not to push, although curiosity keeps her firmly planted on the spot beside him.

An older man walks by, a farmer in overalls with a toothpick in his mouth and the dirtiest cap she's ever seen, once blue, now mostly black.

"John. What do you think that telephone bench is going to go for?" the old man asks.

"For more money than you have, Norm," John says.

"I've got the money, all right, you son-of-a-bitch," Norm mumbles.

"Good," John says. "Put it in your barn so you can call home once in a while."

"Did Jack teach you to harass people like that?" Natha asks.

"As I said, he taught me everything. We were pretty tight."

"I'm sure you were."

"It was quite the love story," he adds. He looks into her eyes, as serious as he can get, she imagines. "I've always wanted to tell someone," he confesses.

"I didn't know him," she says softly. "Only saw him a couple of times at his sales."

"He was a bit of a clown."

"Like you," she says.

"Me? A clown?"

"Yes. You. When you're selling, that is."

"You mean, when I'm performing?"

"It is a performance, isn't it?"

"I try to sell the stuff of the dead and the divorced in an entertaining way."

"You succeed."

"Not with you. You don't laugh at my jokes."

"So, what is it today?" she asks. "Death or divorce?"

"Divorce. Two rich lawyers who were into antiques."

"I suppose their loss is our gain," she says matter-of-factly.

"Jack always said, even if you don't end up divorced, you'll definitely end up dead one day."

"Did he like his work?"

"There was a lot more to the man than the box and the money. Just like me," he says.

"I'm sure there is," she says.

"Actually, I'm about as boring as you can get."

"I doubt that."

"Seriously," he says. "Jack lived a lot more than I have."

"You mean his affair with the schoolteacher?"

"That, and more. I've never had an affair."

"Good for you," she says, regretting the sarcasm in her voice as she soon as she hears it.

"We were virgins when we married."

She laughs.

"That wasn't a joke. I'm serious."

"You finally made me laugh, John Gulliver."

"I'm dead serious. Why don't you believe me?"

"What? You think I'm gullible?"

"I've never been with another woman."

"You're really something."

"Old-fashioned."

"A freak of nature."

"I suppose so, in today's world."

"You are serious, aren't you?"

"Yes," he says firmly. "I'm very serious."

"Oh," she says. "I'm surprised. It's unbelievable, really."

"Not everyone knows that," he confides. "I'd appreciate it if you kept it —"

"I'm not the gossipy type," she assures him. "I don't talk to too many people.'

"I've noticed. Always alone in the crowd, except for the other day," he says. "That's why I feel I can trust you."

"Trust me for what?" she asks.

"You should come out to more sales," he says.

"Why?"

"So you can find some more treasures and we can talk. So I can tell you about Jack and Christina — Cup." ·

"Cup?"

"She was Cup, he was Saucer."

"You're full of shit," she says.

"I'm not!" he protests. "But that is not common knowledge."

"There's too much sentiment around you. You were a virgin. And they called themselves cute little names. You're blowing my mind, John."

"Like I said, there was a reason."

"And you want to tell me?"

"You can't get rid of something until you tell someone about it."

"And you want to get rid of it?"

"Yes, if the truth be known. I do."

"I'm not really into love stories," she says.

"You're a cynic."

"I'm a realist. Affairs are all the same. By the way, who told you my first name?"

"Different people have told me over the years," he answers.

She notices the disappointment in his voice, as if he has been offended by her lack of interest in Jack Callaberry's life, her insensitivity to his need to tell it, not biting, not showing empathy for something that's obviously bothering him. All she needs is another man wanting to unload. If he only knew how often it happens in the Sunrise Motel. He is an innocent, she thinks. And he has been nice. She is curious, if only because Daddy knew Jack Callaberry and said he could understand how a man gets caught up in these things, that the son-of-a-bitch was just too damned nice for his own good.

Still standing beside the medicine cabinet, she thinks of the lives that must have used it.

"Do you ever feel the ghosts, John?"

"Of these antiques, you mean?"

"Yes. Do you feel them?"

"If I did, I'd be done," he says, dismissing Natha's thought.

Of course he would, she thinks. But he doesn't seem haunted by them. She can see that something haunts him, though; she could be the one to release him. But at what cost to herself? Before she gives herself time to consider this, she is telling him that she'd like to know about Jack Callaberry; that if it does him good, she'll listen.

"I'll start low on the cabinet," he says. "Try to keep the price down for you."

He walks off with a bit of a spring in his step; he mounts his box to start the sale. His mouth appears loose and ready for a smile and laughter. She is curious as to what he knows about her, if anything. He didn't ask if she's married. She didn't ask if he has children. It does make sense to her, his wanting to tell a stranger about Jack Callaberry. She understands the needs of men, in particular wanting to talk to someone who is not attached to what they really think or feel.

Why not, she thinks, an hour later, standing in line to pay for the medicine cabinet. She can do with something else to think about. A story other than the narrative that has started to repeat itself in her mind. Besides, she is curious to know what kind of love leaves you hanging from a rope on the second floor of an old mill.

All of her reading of Plath and she still doesn't understand why she put her head in a gas oven, why it came to that.

If only people like Jack Callaberry and Sylvia Plath had known how to push themselves out beyond everything, into the vast blue light.

When she gets to the front of the line to pay, Mary Callaberry's eyes refuse to meet hers. Her blond head is down and she is focused on the money, scratching "medicine cabinet" off her list.

Natha doesn't bother to say hello or make conversation.

At least you know what happened to *your* father, she thinks. Which is worse? Knowing he's dead? Or living with one ear forever cocked to hear his voice again? Over the phone, at the front door, a voice that speaks of return and survival.

SIX

THE RUSH OF THE young blond girl's hair at yesterday's auction sale is still with her the next day. She sifts through the bags of rocks she and Celia have collected in the last couple of years, sorting the special ones to be placed in the ".rock box," as Celia called the medicine cabinet last night, whispering the words as if they held some kind of special magic. Devon complained about its weight, holding it up while Natha made marks on the wall for the brackets that would affix it.

The image of another young blonde has settled into the sediment of her memory. When it emerges, she feels herself on the periphery of it, a young girl herself. All of this seems to have jumped into her life out of blue. She lets a handful of tiny schoolyard stones slip through her fingers back into the bag. Celia, the goddess of small things, collects the tiniest stones she can find, often in the schoolyard when Natha comes to pick her up in the afternoon. She places an assortment of them on the bottom shelf of the medicine cabinet, vowing to keep them always.

Natha doesn't have any rocks from her own childhood, no awards for track meets, no dolls. Did she have dolls? She can't remember. The only thing left is her mother. Daddy gone. Jimmy J. headed west to Alberta when he was only sixteen. The only remaining part of her childhood, her life before Devon and Celia, is Irene. Irene drinking a lake's worth of beggar juice on the shores of Oak Lake in her beloved chair.

She places a fossil rock from the lake on the top shelf of the cabinet.

WHEN SHE WOKE UP, Devon had already left for work at the garage, and so she lay in bed, deciding that she'd had enough of naming the date of each day. Aside from keeping track of when she has to meet with clients, there's no reason to impose such a calendar on her life. It's been a week since she started stamping the day, and it seems her life has sped up since then, like a storm gathering speed. She can hardly believe Celia is six, finishing the first grade. She doesn't want the time with Celia to go by too quickly. She wants to slow it down.

Except for the clock ticking in the kitchen, the house is silent — the kind of silence that befell the house whenever Daddy and Irene went to the Legion and the arguing and the screaming went with them.

She can't decide if she likes the silence today. The clock is making her anxious, as if she is waiting for something. She hasn't waited for anything in a while. Life has been routine. There's nothing she desires. Nothing she is waiting for. Anticipation doesn't dance in her bones.

When the phone rings, she is inclined to let it go, to keep

these hours to herself and the rocks. But the ringing persists and she gives in to the intrusion only to find Stin the glass-blower on the other end, asking to see her tonight, he knows it is last minute but can she?

"Actually, what about now?" he asks.

She has only started with the rocks and Celia is expecting to see them in the rock box after school.

"I can't now. Tonight would be better."

"I have a present for you," Stin says, as if she should be excited and surprised.

She doesn't respond. She doesn't want to show any interest.

"Did you hear me?"

"I heard you," she says. "Meet me outside the motel at nine."

"I made something for you in the hot shop. Aren't you curious?" he asks.

She hangs up.

She's not so sure about this one. He's too attached already, telling her the last time that she's his glory hole now, that he's a different man because of her.

So much shit, she thinks, returning to the rocks, to the pink ones they found along the old railway tracks that run through town. Pink with black spots. Celia calls them "freckle rocks."

"Rocks are medicine," she said to Devon last night. He didn't get it — a medicine cabinet in the living room, not the bathroom, for no other reason than to hold rocks.

"It's not like you have rare gems," he said.

"These are special gems to us," she countered.

"Yeah, Daddy," Celia piped in. "What's gems, Mommy?"

Natha smiles in amusement with the memory of it, how Devon changed his tune and kissed Celia behind the ears and said "special spots," the way she has done it since Celia was a baby, wondering now if Celia will always remember that, if she'll want to keep these rocks all of her life or if they'll just disappear one day and she'll remember other things, like Mommy going out to night school at the last minute, how Mommy said her school was a little different than hers, how Mommy was always going to school.

Detachment starts to set in, a letting go of the sensation of her body.

Stay here, she tells herself. In the silence, and the choosing of rocks and the sight of the medicine cabinet on the wall — how had it ended up here after how many hands?

But the phone —

Now what?

"Natha, I hope you don't mind me calling."

She is suddenly aware of a knot in her back.

"Jules," she says as flatly as she can.

"You still have the same number, Natha."

She sits down on the loveseat, holding the nothing rock. A small, plain, grey rock Celia found on the sidewalk one day. "It's a nothing rock, Mommy," she declared. "Nothing on it. Just a rock."

"I wouldn't have called, Natha," he sighs. "Except it's important."

She rubs the nothing rock between her fingers.

"Nothing's that important that you have to call me, Jules."

"You saw me the other day. I'm not well."

"That's too bad," she says without sympathy.

"I'm dying, Natha. Prostate."

She resists the urge to say, how fitting.

"I need you," he says.

"I don't need you," she replies.

"Can you meet me? So we can talk?"

"Say whatever you have to say now," she answers.

He is silent.

She considers hanging up.

"I didn't expect you to be welcoming," he says softly. "I want to see you one more time."

"What would be the point," she says sharply, "with prostate cancer?"

"That's the whole point. I only want to lie with you, to have you touch me."

"Oh, for Christ's sake, Jules," she snaps.

"Listen. Just listen to me for a minute. I will pay you a lot of money. You're probably not even doing it anymore. But I'll pay you. I've seen you with your daughter — at least I'm assuming it's your daughter."

"Your point?"

"Think of her, what you could do for her with the money. I know you're living on Edward Street again. That your husband only works part time. I doubt you have a lot of money."

"More than you think, Jules."

"Consider it."

"I doubt I'll do that."

"Just one more time, Natha. That's all I'm asking. Just to lie with you, to be with you."

"What's the point?" she shouts into the phone.

"I just want to feel one more time. To see if I still can."

"Don't call me again," she says.

"Please, Natha. Just consider it. I will pay you a lot. Thousands, not hundreds. I don't have anything to lose. Neither do you."

"I have to go now, Jules."

"One more time," he says, and something else she doesn't catch as she hangs up. She heads outside for a cigarette.

The cigarette. The lumber. The lilacs. The grass.

She tells herself she's not going to think of what day this is.

It's a nothing day, she decides, with no desire to remember this as the day that Jules called. She'll erase that. Make it all about the day she filled the rock box with Celia's treasures.

It's not so hard, she thinks. She's been splicing film all her life.

Think of the rocks.

And Celia, the sweet child she gave birth to.

"Christ," she swears quietly. Jules had to bring up Celia.

When Devon comes home for lunch, she tosses it back and forth, to tell or not. The particular scene on the phone with Jules is still running in real time despite her efforts to discard. It was his voice. It hasn't changed. He pleaded with her. He offered her thousands. He uttered the one word he somehow knew would get her attention. "Daughter." How could he have known?

Now Devon is home. She decides she needs him to know, as if the sharing of Jules's phone call might break the recent static between them. She waits until he's finished eating, the two of them opposite each other in the small nook in the kitchen.

"So," he says, as if she just said her mother called and it had no significance. "You should consider it."

"You can't be serious, Devon." If there had at least been some surprise in his voice.

"He doesn't have any kids to leave his money to. Why not give it to you?"

"I cannot be with him, Devon. He's seventy years old!" She's certain this fact alone will make sense. He's always understood her dislike of Jules.

"What makes it any different than when you were fifteen and he was fifty?"

"Christ, give me a break," she says.

"Enlighten me," he says, throwing his arms up into the air.

"I shouldn't have told you."

"Why did you?"

"I thought you'd find it amusing," she lies. "Prostate cancer. He can't even get it up."

"You told me because deep inside you're considering it. You know it's worth considering."

"I told you because I usually tell you everything. I don't want to be with him. I don't want to go back there." *If he would just say no, of course not. No, don't do it.*

"It wouldn't be for long," Devon says, shrugging his shoulders.

"You know, my life might have been different if I hadn't met him."

"What's wrong with your life? Besides, we could use the money."

"It's not your decision," she reminds him.

"You like your things," he says. "Your antiques. And I could use a new truck."

She shakes her head in disbelief. Rising out of her chair, she decides not to respond.

"Not a brand new one," he explains. "A new used one. I can't stand the piece of shit I'm driving now."

CUT TO THE CEMETERY. Having walked out on Devon, she enters it from the bottom of the hill where the graves are newer, where the deaths are more recent. A month ago. A year ago. She prefers the cemetery at night when the dead seem dead, not this display of chiselled stones without shadow and depth. They all seem to be sitting on the surface, the sun too bold and alive for there to be anyone underneath.

One day in the not-too-distant future, Jules will be here.

She can't help but think it. People will remember him as the respected bookstore owner, a fine upstanding citizen of Stirling.

The thought sickens her. She slows her pace. She meanders through the rows, looking at the stones, not retaining any of the names.

If she were to die here, that would put her in the same place as Jules.

That thought sickens her more.

To be dead without this town knowing what happened to her; her life unnoticed by the townspeople, taken for granted, just as the covered bridge at the centre of town. People don't see it anymore. It's just there, like her face, appearing at the bank and the grocery store every once in a while. Before self-pity sets in, she reminds herself it is she who made it this way, who chose to live a muted life and not be noticed or known.

At the top of the hill, she sees the fields of the countryside spreading out to the thin blue horizon. Today, she'd like to escape into it, disappear from the call of the night, just disappear and let Devon think about life without her.

Would it make much difference?

"HE BASICALLY RAPED YOU," Ruthie says when Natha tells her of Jules's call.

They sit on Ruthie's balcony, overlooking the back of liquor store, sipping on straight rye.

"No, he didn't. He propositioned me. I agreed to it."

"You were a child, love."

"I don't see it that way," Natha says. "I was old enough to know what I was doing. Besides, I was never 'just a child.'"

On the way to the school to pick up Celia, her footsteps seem louder than usual, hitting the pavement with resentment. But towards whom? When she sees Celia, greeting her with a handful of tiny stones, she sees one person in her life who knows nothing of any of her reasons for feeling resentment.

It passes, sometime between dinner and bedtime. When she pulls aside the red brocade curtain in her mind and makes the half hour drive to Belleville to the Sunrise Motel, she tells herself she's in charge of everything and always has been — even in her choosing of Devon, of her choosing him to be the one to have a child with. He was detached enough not to smother her and he really hasn't changed; it's business as usual with him. The glassblower gives her a hand-blown glass friendship ball, which she places in the top drawer of the night table in the motel room after he leaves, so someone — maybe a couple — will find it and will consider it a real find, a sign, and sleep peacefully in the airy arms of fate. As if fate had anything to do with it. They won't know it was left by a prostitute who simply couldn't handle a friendly gesture by one of her clients, the come-in-his-own-hand guy. She doesn't want any kind of friendship with him; he's only a means to an end. She's a prostitute who no longer has the friendship of her husband.

She's seeing it now, that Devon only tells her he still loves her and rubs the knot in her back and takes care of the house to keep her going. He didn't even flinch at the sound of Jules's name, never even cracked a joke about his proposition. He was unmoved and pragmatic. It meant more money. A new truck.

There are no stars tonight, the sky is shrouded with cloud. No stars to see when she steps out of the motel room, no stars to tell her the universe hasn't changed and no stars to guide her home as the road seems to wind in a thread of continuity she can hardly bear. She tries to grab an image out of thin air, something to pass through to leave this used-up, spit-out feeling, but she can't fight the road and its steady yellow line, every mile bringing her closer to home.

SEVEN

Natha is beginning to feel how a person can get lost in her own life, waking up as she did this morning to memories of Jules's hands on her and Devon's reaction to his call and the long, drawn-out sex with Stin, feeling every minute of it again while making breakfast, showering, touching her body with soap to erase his calloused fingering.

Before she left the house to walk Celia to school, she added a volume of Virginia Woolf's diaries to the pile in the living room, plunked it down on top of Sylvia Plath's journals and Anaïs Nin's diaries as if to say "And you too." She'd rather be lost in their lives than to keep feeling her own. Than to keep feeling, period. She had it right last night on the way home from the motel — — used up, spit out.

She walks along Church towards the auction at the end of the street, trying to push herself out beyond everything, inhaling and exhaling, expanding the small, feeling, affected woman fetally curled in her stomach. She doesn't want John Gulliver picking up the scent of her insides. She only wants to let off mild interest in the story of Jack Callaberry and the love affair that killed him. She thought of it when she decided she didn't have the patience to sit down and read.

The small, fetal, used-up, spit-out woman inside already made a mistake this morning, turning to her six-year-old daughter for proof of love, whispering, singing "Mama-loves-the-baby" into her ear, forcing Celia to respond "Baby-loves-the-Mama," the way they used to sing to each other when Celia was younger.

Christ, she thinks, she shouldn't have done that, forcing Celia to revert to babyhood. Now, thinking about it, a heavy feeling of anxiety and shame stops her breath. Celia didn't giggle like she used to when she heard her mother sing it. She looked at Natha with surprise and then worry before she sang back. Natha realizes that she must have seen need in her mother's eyes.

"Fuck," Natha swears, stiffening her back. "Fuck."

She walks on, taking note of the colour of each house until the emotions caused by her realization are gone. She counts the house numbers, considers the types of front doors, until she arrives at the red brick bungalow where the sale is being held. Several cars and trucks are already lined up close by, the bratwurst guy setting up his barbeque in the driveway.

"Everything's in the back," he tells her.

She walks through a carport full of boxes and sees John Gulliver at the very back of a large yard, standing with his arms crossed, talking to two men, flanked by antiques on either side. One she recognizes as the long-haired picker she saw at the sale at King's Mill. John sees her as she enters the yard; he stares intensely, and uncrosses his arms as if he is about to come towards her. But he stays with the two men. She turns her attention to the stretch of tables set up along the back of the house, covered with trinkets and tableware. She feels she is wasting time pretending to be interested — someone's silverware polished and laid out after how many decades of meals? The turkey platter and punch bowl and the small coffee cups, the kind that come with a set no one ever uses. Then the array of mismatched coffee mugs, no doubt only out here because someone has died, their fingerprints still visible on the stainless steel pots and pans. Christmas decorations, which strike her as too personal to be included. Crystal ashtrays and a collection of pocket watches, one with hands in keeping with today's time, and she can't help but find the irony in its accuracy, ticking away past its owner's life.

The body may be dead and buried, but here lies the estate of the recently departed, the final undressing of a life in the objects collected and used. The atmosphere is split between nostalgia and anticipation as the crowd increases with people looking for a bargain.

John makes his way across the yard, passing her with barely a nod, his body moving with a mission. He walks into the house. She wanders farther into the yard and sits herself in an antique rocker, lights a cigarette, and waits. If he's not back in five minutes, if he doesn't come to her, she will leave. John, the virgin-man, the one-woman-man. If he only knew how she could break him of that, she is thinking as he reappears outside the house and makes his way towards her, looking as intensely at her as before, but now with a bit of a smile.

"Sorry for walking past like that," he says. "Someone tipped me that a family member was going to play games today."

"What kind of games?"

"Bid on things just to raise the price. I run an honest sale. No one gets away with that shit with me. Come on, let's talk over there," he says, pointing to a corner near the garden shed at the back, under tall pine trees.

"If the price goes higher, I assume you make more money," she says.

"My reputation is worth more," he answers, crossing his arms again. "So, you came. For the sale? Or the story?"

"There isn't anything here I'm interested in."

They stand side by side, peering over the steadily increasing crowd.

"You're married, aren't you?" he asks.

"I never told you that, and I don't wear a ring."

"That tells me you have an open mind," he says.

"Actually," she says, "I never liked the feeling of it on my finger."

"How long?" he asks.

"Long enough," she answers. "But this isn't about me."

"I've been married a long time too. I was fourteen when I met Mary. She was twelve. When Jack started pulling back from his family, he made me promise I'd be good to her."

"And you have, from what you've told me."

A strand of hair blows into her eye and before she can brush it away, John gently puts it back in place.

"I think I trust you," he says. "And I'm usually a good judge of character."

"You base your judgment on very little, John."

"When you spend over thirty years of your life in crowds, you get a feeling for people," he says.

"Over thirty years," she repeats. "That makes you —"

"Forty-six. I started at fourteen with Jack on weekends. He was like the father I always wished I had."

"You didn't have a father?"

"Oh, I had one. His only form of communication was this," he says, holding up a fist.

"So you hung out with Jack when you were young?"

"Hung out, learned everything. I worked with him full-time right after high school, then he died and I kept going."

"Did he leave a note?" she asks.

"Would you believe hundreds of notes?" he answers.

"To who?"

"To me. But we're getting ahead of ourselves."

"Hundreds? Why hundreds?"

He turns to face her.

"Let me ask you something. Why do you want to know about this?"

"You said you needed to tell someone."

"So, you're doing it for me?"

"I heard about Jack's suicide when I was young. How many years ago was it?"

"Twenty. He was fifty-seven."

"Seems everything started twenty years ago for you."

"Too much started twenty years ago," he says.

"I'm just curious, to answer your question."

"Is it the death part or the love part you're curious about, Natha?"

"A love that kills you? I find it hard to believe," she says dismissively.

"But you're standing here," he says, grinning.

"You strike me as naive," she tells him, boldly. *What's the point of skirting around?* she thinks. Mr. Honest in business and in marriage. She could almost laugh, but that would belittle him. She lets her statement fall on him like the hot morning air; the tiny beads of sweat under his eyes almost look like tears.

He genuinely looks hurt, and kicks at the ground with one foot, his head lowered.

"I take it that's an insult," he says eventually, not a trace of the clown or the performer in him. A boy, she thinks, remembering the boy he was when she went with Daddy to one of Jack Callaberry's sales and John stood beside him, learning. Now a man with a story and she's just knocked his ego. It is disturbing to see his soul so exposed. It's like she let the air out of him.

"Being cynical is not all it's cracked up to be," she tells him, jokingly, trying to clean up the mess. He stops kicking the ground and gives her a warm smile. His muscular body fills up again and she notices the lines around his mouth — from the hours in the sun, no doubt. Creases of the trade. Or from keeping it shut all these years about Jack.

In this corner of the backyard, under these pines, the crowd far enough away to make her feel apart from it, she feels removed from Jules's phone call and Devon's reaction and the sticky needs of men in the motel. All of these are somewhere on the other side of town, on the other side of her day.

"Now that that's all out of the way," John sighs, "we can either proceed or go our separate ways."

She likes the fact he has bounced back with a response as direct as her comment about his naivety. And if not this, then what? She'll be left to the lives of Sylvia Plath and Virginia Woolf. She already knows how they turned out. She'll be left with Devon and Jules and their predictable words and gestures and she's already brought an end to that story. She won't go to Jules, not even for money for Celia's future.

"What was it they called each other?" she asks John, as clear a sign as she can give him that she's choosing to proceed.

"Cup and Saucer," he says. "Christina collected them at Jack's sales. They didn't stand here at a sale, like we are. They passed notes. She was Cup. He was Saucer."

Mary Callaberry waves from the carport.

"She doesn't have a clue about the notes," John says. "I made a promise to Jack."

"You made a lot of promises to that man."

"More than you know."

"So tell me, then," she says.

"Right now I have to go and help her set up," he says. "I'll see you again?"

"Yes," she answers.

"You should come earlier next time. Give us more time."

"I have a young daughter to get to school," she says.

"Oh, that's right," he says, as if he already knows. She can't remember taking Celia to any auctions.

"I could come earlier to a sale on a Saturday," she suggests.

"I have one tomorrow," he says.

"That's right. Tomorrow is Saturday," she says, realizing she hasn't been thinking of what day it is, feeling like she's forgotten today is Friday even though she knew it was Friday this morning when she remembered he had an auction today. This short-term memory loss disturbs her; life seems to be picking up speed before she can process things, put them in their proper places in her mind, or throw them out over some cliff in her imagination, into a wild river that carries them into an ocean, out into nowhere. That's what she needs to do with Jules. Throw him over the cliff, let him drown in an ocean. Then again, she thinks, he's dying. She wonders how long he has. He didn't say.

"Do you have children?" she asks, switching gears.

"One, but he died at three weeks," he says. His grey-green eyes become dull. She notices the creases around them. These aren't caused by the sun; he's aged faster than he should. She should have noticed his eyes before, the way they match his mood, sparkling, practically jumping when he's joking, then melancholy like now. She's looked in the eyes of enough men to know the ones that carry some great weight on their shoulders. That's why the sex has to be in a dark room. She can't handle seeing their eyes, to know there's a life behind them.

"I should go," he says, before she has the chance to say "I'm sorry," leaving her to digest what he has just said, under the pines in the corner, someone else's life to think about now.

The spot beside her, where he was just standing, still feels taken up by his presence. Beside it she sees the long-haired picker as he spits on a dead man's lawn. A young couple try out the dead man's couch, bouncing up and down testing its support. The smell of bratwurst fills the air. She passes John and Mary in the carport, laughing about something; John, looking animated. She can feel him becoming clown and honest auctioneer and she's sure he will do his best to sell all the possessions of the deceased, whose name she cannot recall from the newspaper. *Piper,* she thinks, and she can practically hear the hands on Piper's pocket watch ticking on one of the tables, counting the minutes until the sale starts and the dispersal of his earthly possessions begins.

REACHING INTO A DRAWER of her dresser later for her bathing suit, she notices her wedding ring on top of her dresser in an opened box. A small, antique, white-gold ring with a half-carat diamond. She lied when she told John Gulliver she doesn't wear it because she doesn't like the feel of it on her finger. She wore it for the first year of her marriage, but it interrupted her ability to dissociate at the Sunrise and so she put it away. Devon understood and didn't mind, and said their sacred marriage was tied by something greater than a piece of jewellery. It was like a knee-jerk reaction to the occasion for her, getting married as they did in a small ceremony by a Unitarian minister in the living room. The ring was the only thing that made the wedding seem real. Only Irene and Clyde were there. Devon's family, fine, upstanding citizens who worked for the government in Ottawa, were estranged from him; they didn't like his bohemian ideas or his pot smoking or his lack of ambition. Irene and Clyde sat on the loveseat and drank and acted as if it was just another visit.

Natha found the ring at an antique show in the Quinte Mall in Belleville. The dealer said it was from the 1930s. She tried the ring on and it fit and she took that as a good omen, wondering about the life of the woman who wore it before. She could sense her and what she sensed was loss of some kind, that the ring had been abandoned for a long time.

On her own wedding day, when Devon placed the ring on Natha's finger, she didn't feel a burst of love or some great sense of belonging. It was just a token of how she'd spend the next part of life. Married. A bookmark in the next chapter of her existence. She still felt separate.

The first thing she notices when she arrives at Irene's for a swim is the round wooden candy dish sitting on the old sewing machine table near the front door. She lifts the lid and sees that it is half full of chocolate rosebuds that are whitening with age.

"I forget," she says to Irene. "Where did you get this?"

"At a woodcarvers' show in Belleville a million years ago, when I was still with your father."

"I don't remember it," she tells Irene.

"I never used it then. The only reason I use it now is because I never used it when I was married to your father. I threw out all the things I used in that marriage when I moved in with Clyde."

"Even those tiny felt elves you used to hang on the mirror in the living room at Christmastime? I'd like those if you have them. They're the only thing I remember about Christmas from my childhood."

"They're gone," Irene says, dismissively. "So is the mirror. Why are they important now?'

"I don't know," Natha answers. "I just thought of them now."

She doesn't say it to Irene, but there was a lot tied up in

those red-and-green felt elves with their tiny white felt hats with bells on them. They were so innocent-looking with their childlike faces. She used to put her hopes for a good Christmas into them: that Daddy wouldn't get so drunk he'd knock the Christmas tree over, as he did one year, punching it instead of Irene during an argument. She didn't wish for presents. She wished for peace. She remembers that now, how she put her faith in those two tiny inanimate objects, as if they had some kind of magical spirit to pull off a Christmas miracle. How old was she then? Not much taller than the furniture, she imagines. Maybe younger than Celia.

A flash of the young blond-haired girl comes to her as she stands near the sewing machine with the candy dish, the blond hair rushing by. The floor suddenly feels wavy and Natha is off balance. She reaches out to lay a hand on the table.

"What is wrong with you?" Irene asks.

"Just a little dizzy," she tells her.

"Don't tell me you're pregnant or something," Irene barks.

The thought had never entered Natha's mind. Impossible, she thinks. She steadies herself, dismisses the idea of it. It's something else. A dizzy, agitated sensation. Fearful even.

"You'll have to give the candy dish to Celia someday," she says to her mother. "It's the first thing she goes to when she comes here. But would you put some fresh chocolate in it?"

"Do you think some wooden dish means anything to a child?"

"The elves meant something to me," Natha says, hating that an accusation enters her tone of voice, that these things matter. She won't ever throw out Celia's rocks or the icicles they made together out of blue Play-Doh last Christmas for the tree.

The dizzy feeling passes. But the elves, the candy dish, Piper's ticking pocket watch, and John Gulliver's grey-green eyes stay with her as she sits outside in her bathing suit by the shoreline with Irene, who is drinking from a large white mug with the saying *Everything tastes better with cat hair in it!*

"Where did you get that mug?" she asks Irene.

"Stedman's. Why?"

"You've had it a long time."

"I got it a year before Goose died. It reminds me of him."

Goose was the name of Irene's grey tabby.

The cat is dead. The mug lives on.

Christ, Natha thinks, if that mug ever ends up on a table at an auction — the things people won't know. How many years it's served as the first-few-drinks-of-the-day mug, never seeing the light of day with coffee or tea, but vodka and orange or a Bloody Caesar.

"What time is it, Mother?"

"Almost noon."

The mug will be replaced by a glass and some rye soon.

Almost noon. June what? Friday. She knows that much. Friday, the auction Saturday tomorrow and maybe she will go to another auction.

"Remember Jack Callaberry?" she says to Irene.

"Of course. What? Do you think I'm forgetting things?"

"No. Just what did you know about him?"

Irene lights a cigarette, takes a long drag.

"I didn't know him. I only went to a few auctions of his. Your father liked him. Said he was a straight shooter. But I guess he had everyone fooled."

"I've been to a couple of auctions recently."

"Acquiring more stuff?" Irene says sarcastically.

"I saw Buddy Francis at one of them," Natha tells her, knowing it will push a button, but she puts it out there anyway. Seeing Buddy that day, and these flashes of the young blond-haired Darlene.

"I never did like that bastard," Irene says into her mug just before another sip.

"You mean, how he got Daddy drunk all the time?"

"You've got to stop that, Natha," Irene snaps.

"Stop what?"

"Stop calling him Daddy," she says sternly.

"Sorry," Natha says, not meaning it, but wanting to keep Irene talking, about Buddy. "Was I ever alone with Buddy when I was young?" she asks.

Irene gives her a long stare.

"Why are you so deep in the past? Why are you asking me this? About Christmas decorations and Jack Callaberry and Buddy bloody Francis?"

"It's just that I saw him —"

"So, you saw him. So what? He was a bad drunk. No wonder his wife left him."

"Was I ever at his place?"

"You may have gone over there once or twice. Mostly you played with Darlene at our place. Don't tell me you don't remember that?"

"I don't."

"What did you buy at these auctions?"

"A desk for Celia. Do you know Jules Moore is dying?"

"That's old news."

"I didn't know until I ran into him the other day at Stedman's."

"He was a good client of yours for a few years," Irene says. "He paid you well. I told you he was dying a long time ago."

"No, you didn't."

"I thought I did. Maybe I just meant to. I remember thinking it, of telling you."

"It doesn't matter, Mother."

"Christ, aren't we just full of the past today," Irene says cheerfully, standing up. "I'm going to get another one. Do you want one?"

"No thanks," Natha answers, lighting a cigarette, exhaling agitation. Irene downs the rest of her drink and heads inside for the next one. She'll return with a glass of rye instead of the cat-hair mug.

"Jesus Christ, it's hot today," Irene yells out just before she disappears, leaving Natha with only the sight of her empty lounge chair, with its painted white steel frame and floral cushion, no doubt sopping up Irene's avoidance and denial, not to mention her urine. She wonders how much it would go for at an auction. Do the things of the sick and the bitter bring darkness to a new owner's life?

She shakes herself loose from the trance of the chair, feeling beads of sweat between her breasts. She thinks of John Gulliver, standing for hours on his wooden box, selling the last of the possessions of another life, how his soul will be camouflaged during the process, how he is just down the street from Celia's school, sweet Celia, sitting in a school room without air conditioning, the windows open, noise from the street, and Devon with black hands, wiping his nose under someone's hood, thankful he doesn't have to work more than two days a week, while around the corner and over two streets is Jules, shrinking in the darkness of his bedroom and the one object on his dresser that was there in those years with him — the small portrait of his wife in a cream-coloured fabric frame, her rosary hanging on one side.

She could be his object for one night, take him for all he's worth.

She can't remember when her next gig is or what she had for breakfast this morning, can't remember going to sleep last night, or how long it took until she did. Maybe it's just the heat, she thinks, this inability to remember the immediate. Didn't she promise to take Celia to the park tonight? She rises from her chair and walks to the water's edge. Sensation in the body is what she needs to stop all this feeling. She steps into the lake, the water warm and soothing and timeless, she swims into it and feels a return to a safe and loving womb; if only, she thinks, to be yet again so free of the things that entangle her.

BEFORE NATHA LEAVES HER mother's, after she has dried off and changed back into her clothes, Irene presents her with an aluminum tray Natha made in her last year at school. It is a large, round, silver tray with crimped edges and has a pattern of pine cones on it.

"Here," Irene says, handing it over. "I kept this because you made it for me. Take it home with you. Something from your youth."

THE FIRST THING SHE sees when she gets home is Devon's guitar sitting by the kitchen door in its scuffed leather case. It is just after one in the afternoon and the sky has darkened again, turning grey and overcast, threatening, making the white room dark and dull. The clock on the wall seems louder to her, the tap dripping slightly. Devon never shuts it off properly. He is obviously home and hasn't gone back to work after lunch. She is about to call out his name when he appears in the doorway, under the ceramic sun on the wall just above. He looks like a kid who's about to get into trouble, who has his shoulders ready for fire.

"What's up?" she says, casually.

"I'm heading off to Barb's," he answers.

"What about work?"

"Taking the afternoon off."

"Off?" she says. "To see Barb?"

"She was in this morning and we got talking and you know how it goes."

He looks at the tap dripping and tightens the handle until it stops.

"What did you tell your boss?"

"That the heat was getting to me."

Natha gestures towards the guitar.

"Are you going to serenade her?"

It comes out more like an accusation than a question, but she doesn't care. She is pissed off that he is taking time off work to do this.

"You must have been with your mother this morning," he says to her, grinning with cockiness.

What's the point, she thinks, going down this path with him. She opens the fridge to get some Perrier.

"You haven't exactly been amorous lately," he continues.

"I thought you wanted a new truck," she says. "If you want one, you should be working for it."

A huge smile crosses Devon's face.

"Good one," he says. "That's really good."

She reaches for a glass from the cupboard, brushing his shoulder as she does it. He hasn't mentioned Jules's proposition since she told him, but she knows it's still on his mind, that it won't just go away. He's just been waiting for the right time to bring it up it in a way that makes perfect sense to her. Anything for the money that doesn't cost him anything.

"If you prefer I don't take the guitar, I won't," he tells her, placing a hand on her shoulder while she pours the Perrier into the glass. He places his other hand on her other shoulder and begins massaging her, running his fingers down until he finds the knot in her back. The last time he pulled his guitar out for her she felt like she was just putting time in listening to him. It wasn't that long ago. When was that? she thinks. A week ago, two weeks? It appealed to her the first few years they were together, but then again, she was stoned as much as he was. Now, she practically dreads him bringing it out. Who cares, she thinks, if he takes the thing with him. He can even sing their song — "Stacks of Gold" — for Barb for all she cares today. It's just a piece of wood with some strings.

"I need to get into the shower," she says, stepping away from him. "Have a good time. And make sure you come home tonight. I'm heading out early in the morning to an auction. You'll have to get up with Celia."

"Okay," is all he says, even though she knows the fact she's going to another auction is sitting there at the end of his tongue. He walks right by the guitar, grabbing only a case of beer on the way out.

She could see it as a sign of respect for her, that he still places her above all the rest, but she doesn't want to feel his love in any way, not when he's still willing to walk out the door.

By the time she's finished showering, a heavy rain has begun to fall. It sounds like an unleashed flood of tears, she thinks as she dresses; the world weeping over our material lives, our silly attachment to guitars we no longer want to hear and Christmas elves that never brought a miracle on Christmas Day. Let it go, she thinks, let it go. The phone rings on the washstand in the corner of the bedroom.

"Natha, don't hang up," Jules says at the other end. "I'm only calling to tell you I'll pay just for you to come over and talk to me. Just talk about what I called about last time."

His voice is raspy and needy.

"We've been over this," she says, looking at the clock. She has to go and get Celia in a minute. She'll have to take the car, she decides.

"Just to talk. A thousand dollars," he says.

What is it with this day? she thinks, rubbing in some lotion she missed before on her right leg, letting the silence between herself and Jules linger a while, trying to be here in the moment in her own room, not in his living room at his mahogany desk where his olive green rotary dial phone used to sit, which he wouldn't give up for a new one. She used to call Irene from his house to say that he needed extra cleaning that day, that she'd be home late. She wants to ask him if he's still using that phone but that would indicate connection to him, to their past.

"I'll think about it," is all she says.

"You do that," he replies.

"Goodbye," she says.

"For now," he says.

There are objects of desire, she thinks, a man or a woman, and then there are objects of another kind. Some sit in the corner of a shop of antiques. The rest, if not dutifully passed down to the next generation, are sold at an auction. A hand is raised and money passed and the story of a cup and saucer is lost and forgotten.

Never mind that Celia greets her inside the school with a paper fairy house she made today during art. All the will in the world to keep it, cherish it always, may well dwindle when her house is overrun with these treasures and she's forced one day to discard them. What to keep, what to throw out?

She gets a plastic bag from the teacher to carry the fairy house home in the relentless rain. She didn't see this storm coming, not the fury it has landed with. She dresses Celia in the raincoat and rubber boots she has brought with her. They make a mad dash for the car and, once home, they sit huddled together on the couch, Celia burrowing into her arms, frightened by the blaring thunder and lightning. Natha is certain she's never heard it so loud before. The paper fairy house sits dry and safe on the long, low table in front of them.

"What if lightning hits our house, Mommy?"

"It won't," Natha assures her, rubbing her back, kissing the top of her head.

"You can't go to school in this, Mommy."

"I'm staying home tonight. Don't worry."

"How will Daddy get home from work?"

"He's working late. It'll be over by the time he comes home. Don't worry."

"I need Shaggy Bear," Celia says in a small voice.

"I'll go and get him," Natha offers.

"No! I don't want to be alone."

"C'mon. We'll go together."

Celia is hesitant, but she takes Natha's hand and the two climb the stairs to a higher level of noise, the rain pelting on the roof of the house. The first thing Natha notices is that the roof has leaked in Celia's bedroom, in the corner near her small white bookcase.

"You stay here, on your bed, with Shaggy. I need to go and get a pail."

"Hurry, Mommy."

Natha quickly checks the other rooms upstairs. There's a leak near the outside wall in the guestroom. Her room and the bathroom seem fine. She returns with a large pot and a pail and places them under the swelling, leaking plaster of the ceilings. Celia insists on returning to the living room, to the couch, under a blanket, just the two of them.

As frightening as the storm is for Celia, Natha is thankful for the time alone with her, to focus on what is real and alive: Celia's small body, living, breathing, expressing itself in tight hugs and little whimpers of fright. There, there, Natha says with her hands. She realizes this is how she likes it best, just her and Celia in the house. Devon never had any problem with them becoming three. It is Natha who feels as though she became two-thirded — she and Celia, separate from Devon. She has never felt it so deeply as she does on this stormy afternoon, while Devon is no doubt trying to storm Barb's life with his philosophy and his penis. What she feels today for him, or doesn't feel, makes it all the harder to understand how anyone can love so deeply that they kill themselves over it.

She can't imagine love at all.

Except for Celia.

"You can't get rid of something until you tell someone," John Gulliver said to her at that auction sale where it was raining and he walked her from her car to the medicine cabinet. She'd like to tell him now that there have never been any real storms in her relationship with Devon, nor sunrises either. That the routine of their days is what they've had, with nothing but expectations to remain the same. Dare she step off of the path that has been the steady line in her life? She can't imagine it, handing herself over to another. She didn't veer when Daddy left and never came back. Is that what she wants to tell John? That is what frightens her the most. That she's never felt enough to veer? Just to say it would be defeat and defeat isn't allowed, only steady survival. In the end, what does any of it matter, she thinks. Everything is disposable.

EIGHT

NATHA SOFTLY PULLS CELIA's hair back and kisses the special spot behind her ear. There's a kind of purity, she thinks, in showing love while someone sleeps with no expectation of response. It's just given. The air is cooler after the storm and a breeze blows lightly through the window beside Celia's bed, brushing Natha's face with an alertness that isn't conducive to sleep. The still-swollen ceiling, dripping water into a steel pot in the corner of the room, keeps her wound up. It sounds like the delayed ticking of the clock. She considers going into her own room, but that means lying next to Devon, who has only just returned home and might still be awake.

She doesn't want the interaction.

She wraps an arm around Celia's small body and hides under the covers. She stays under until breathing becomes difficult and then she pulls the covers down from her face. The light from a streetlamp filters in enough for her to see the shadows and outlines of everything in the room, all the objects of childhood, including the ridiculously large stuffed animals sitting on top of the wardrobe given to Celia by Irene. There are Barbies and their accessories filling the basket-like bassinet from Celia's infancy. Then there is the rolltop desk on the other side of the room, with colouring books stacked on top.

Natha still senses the woman from the 1930s; she pictures her, her hand moving gracefully across paper as she writes a letter, a woman of integrity and dignity. She wishes for Celia to have the qualities of the letter-writing woman more than her own qualities of resilience and resourcefulness. She doesn't want Celia to have to be resilient against anything, doesn't want her to know hardship. She wishes for her a charmed, dignified life. If she has it right, if there was such a woman who once sat at the desk.

Sometimes she wishes Celia wasn't so innocent and so in awe of her, believing her mother to be an educated woman. How long can she put that over her child? Celia telling her she's such a good reader, that she must be good at school. The lie of it all, in a room with the always-be-honest Shaggy Bear up there on the wardrobe.

Another drop hits the pot and her feet hit the floor to leave.

She doesn't want to be alone with herself. She heads downstairs for the company of Sylvia and Virginia and Anaïs. In the soft glow of the living room she can't make up her mind whose life is the life she needs right now. She scrambles hurriedly through their stories, trying to remember a segment where something was said that could help settle her pulse, deflect the one story that is emerging from pages still unwritten — the story of her own life that sits in her chest, heavy and making its way up. These books she knows so well, she can even guess on which side of the page something resonated with her, but they only serve to remind her of the escape they gave her in Jules's house.

Now the roof of her own house is leaking.

It will cost money to fix it.

She doesn't want to touch the Come What May Account at the bank.

Here she sits, holding books written decades ago, facing the question of where the money will come from, just as Sylvia did and Virginia did; Anaïs, too, struggling to pay the bills. At least they were pursuing art, she thinks, while she sits here contemplating talking to Jules about sex for a thousand dollars to pay for the roof. "Just to talk," he said.

She may not have put it down on paper but it's still there — the cloudy day with October trees tapping the windows in Jules's bedroom. She was dusting the top of his dresser, the portrait of his wife, wiping dust off the rosary beads, running the cloth over and under the handles.

"Pull open the top right drawer," Jules said from the doorway.

She didn't know he'd been standing there watching her.

She did as he instructed. She saw the box of condoms. When she looked back at him, a smile had swept across his face, under his reading glasses. He was holding a copy of *Lolita*.

She could ask Irene to help with the roof, but she knows where that will lead, a skittish, roundabout, said-but-not-said acknowledgement of what Natha does for a living. Clear, concise conversation eludes her mother.

Sometimes she wishes Irene would just come out with it. It would be better if she did. At least then Natha wouldn't feel invisible, Irene saying earlier that Jules was a good client, as if it was all about housework.

These women, still alive on the page, all wrote about their mothers. She knows their stories. Who will ever know hers?

Jules said his wife was like Virginia Woolf, unable to enjoy sex with a man.

He was older than Daddy.

Now she remembers that time in the library with Ruthie, listening to Sylvia Plath's voice. She was reading her poem, "Daddy," sounding like a grave, old child who never could forget.

What could she ever write about Ray Cole?

In her journals, Sylvia said she wished she could find someone else's life to write about other than her own.

Take mine, Natha thinks, but the language will bore you. Too many *fuck me baby*s, the repetition of it.

She sets the books back down on the coffee table and picks up the aluminum tray next to them, the clock from the kitchen ticking loudly. She tries to remember making it. She remembers the tech shop classroom smelled burnt. She remembers how hard it was to crimp the edges. She thinks she cut herself. She can't remember how she put the pattern of pine cones on it.

She holds it waiting for something of herself to come.

Fifteen.

After Daddy.

Before Jules.

After a while, she goes outside to have a cigarette. Some of the smoke gets in her left eye and it tears up. She wipes it, but it continues to tear, her eye sore and tired and it almost starts. Christ, she thinks, I could cry right now — really cry — but she steadies herself against it.

This, she thinks, is what Sylvia would write about: how nothing came while holding the tray and then, moments later, something as simple as cigarette smoke in the eye almost brought on a cloudburst of tears.

When she goes back inside, she turns on her computer. Tonight, the blank screen seems to call her. She stares at the small black line flashing at the top of the page, waiting for her to start.

Where does a person start?

She can hear Virginia Woolf recording another bout of depression and her problem with the fidgets turning to her work on a novel as she lay in bed with a fever. And Sylvia Plath anxiously awaiting word from *The New Yorker* about some poems she sent in and setting a gruelling schedule for herself to write more, read more. And Anaïs Nin lamenting profoundly about her discoveries of the unconscious and the need to turn to the self. And it seems to Natha that they *had* something to say; their voices crystallized in her mind far more than her own. Leonard Woolf and Ted Hughes and all the men in Anaïs's life are known to her better than most of the men she has fucked at the Sunrise. Years lived and buried by her own mind, behind a red brocade curtain, and under the stars and whatever else she could think of to keep herself from feeling. She's always relied on her mind to put her someplace else and realizes now she has all but made herself disappear. Thirty-five and she cannot recall who she was at fifteen, after Daddy left, before she slept with Jules, when she made an aluminum tray and gave it to her mother. The memory of feeling escapes her.

Who stood there today at the auction?

Who swam in the lake?

How she can feel the life of a woman who once sat at a rolltop desk and not feel herself?

She Googles *the secret life of objects* and lands on a site for a Dr. David Riddell in California, a scientist who studies parapsychology. It seems odd, until she clicks on one of his articles and briefly scans sentences about probing the far reaches of consciousness and psi phenomena, the perception of objects beyond the range of ordinary sense, and that one of the most surprising discoveries of modern physics is that objects aren't as separate as they seem. It feels off-track to be reading this, her mind taking over, linking to other thoughts, breaking the flow of where she was going, loosening her from her own life. That's the way it was when she was young reading Plath and Woolf and Nin in Jules's house, immersed in literary lives in other worlds while she was living with a drunk mother and fucking the bookstore owner in a small, rural town.

What would this Dr. David Riddell think of hearing from a hooker in Stirling, Ontario who cannot feel her own life but can feel the lives of others in objects from the past?

Why not? she thinks, and sends a quick email asking him why this happens.

There, she thinks, she'll never hear from him anyway.

There, it's gone. All the emotion of this night.

She heads into the kitchen for a glass of water and sees a note left on the counter by Devon. He forgot to tell her that Ruthie called this morning while she was out at the auction, that Ruthie was going to the hospital. She was dancing and fell and her shoulder might be broken.

I'm sorry I forgot to tell you.

Three a.m. and she's pissed now at Devon and returns to Celia's room. She'll have to go to Ruthie first thing. The story of Jack Callaberry and his love affair will have to wait. And there's the roof to tend to.

The drops have stopped, like the brush-up with her own life tonight, over now. Eyes dry and tearless, she closes them under a ceiling that no longer weeps; fading now, she drifts to sleep.

NINE

THE CLAMPS OF INDECISION are tight around her forehead in the morning. Walking to Ruthie's apartment, she feels as though her body is pushing through mud to get her there, even though the air is cool and light, the sun quietly above her, not shouting any particular direction to take.

Devon didn't say much when she told him about the roof. He expects she'll take care of it. She didn't tell him about Jules's call last night and doesn't plan to. More and more it seems there's no reason to tell Devon about what is going on in her life, the lived moments outside of him and their sacred marriage. Jules. And John Gulliver. And Buddy Francis. And the hayfields and memories of Daddy and this little blond-haired girl who rushes by in her mind. All she said about the aluminum tray when Devon asked about it was that Irene gave it to her. He didn't notice her name etched in the back by her fifteen-year-old hand.

She walks along Edward Street with imbalance in her step. She used to know what her life was by not thinking about it.

She makes a right onto Wellington and follows what seems like an unusual amount of early morning traffic, the cars turning onto Nancy Street ahead, until she sees it — a yard sale three doors down. It makes her think of the auction sale and John Gulliver, how she won't be able to talk to him today. Now that she can't, she wants to — more than she did before. He may be some naive country boy, but they're not so far apart. They both perform for the money and deal with the widowed and the divorced and the dispossessed. Impulse makes her want to go to him, but Ruthie needs her. She walks on to Ruthie's apartment, split down the middle, then decides to stop and seek comfort in someone else's things. She rationalizes that Ruthie will just be getting up now, that she may as well give her some time.

She turns around and heads back to Nancy Street, to rummage and to release the clamps around her forehead. She can count on getting lost in the tangible distraction of objects. She sees it all as she approaches. A driveway lined with boxes and bicycles and racks of clothes, a table full of dishes, some crystal glinting in the sun, the horde of people — How much for this? Will you take two for that?

The house is small — a bungalow with pale green siding. She has never actually walked down this short street before, a mix of bungalows and renovated wartime houses, close together, everyone's lawns impeccable, June gardens flowering. Such an intimate street, she thinks, compared to the sprawling older homes of Edward Street. You can't live on a street like this and avoid your neighbours. A narrow street without sidewalks.

She starts to sift through boxes of books, a peculiar mix of commercial novels and literary classics.

"Good morning," a woman says from behind her.

Natha turns to see the deli woman from the grocery store, the one she has seen walking with her daughter, Celia's age.

"Are you looking for anything in particular?" the woman asks while Natha takes her in. Her own age, she estimates, a little shorter, thinner, with blond hair down to her shoulders and bright blue eyes, a little too wholesome for her liking.

"No, just looking. It's an awful lot of stuff to come out of one house."

"Most of it is my mother's," she says. She extends a hand. "I'm Deborah."

"Natha. So, this is your house?"

"We just moved here a couple of months ago from Cobourg. I see you on the street sometimes with your daughter and in Foodland."

"The deli."

"I couldn't find anything else."

"Who's the reader? You or your mother?"

"My mother was," Deborah answers sadly.

"I'm sorry," Natha says.

"No. She's not dead, just blind."

"Well, I'm sorry about that too."

Some antique gold leaf frames, leaning against the corner of the house, catch Natha's eye.

"I'm interested in those frames there," she says.

"My mother collected antiques," she says. "They are so old. I never knew what to put in them."

"I took some photos of a friend recently for a birthday present. They'd be perfect for them."

The two walk over to the frames, excusing themselves through the crowd.

"We should get our daughters together for a play date," Deborah suggests.

"Sure," Natha says. "What are you asking for these?"

Deborah picks up three frames and hands them to Natha.

"You know what?" she says. "Just take these three with you."

"No," Natha says, emphatically. "Seriously. What do you want for them?"

"Nothing," Deborah insists. "Just take them. I'll make enough money off the rest of this shit today," she says, grinning as if the word *shit* has just cut through some ice.

"I owe you," Natha tells her, with no idea how she can repay the favour and not necessarily wanting to.

"Just drop by sometime," Deborah says.

"I will," Natha says, feeling obligated. She would rather have paid for the frames and be done with it. Now there are expectations, and the way Deborah the deli woman said "shit" seemed forced, like she said it to dispel any ideas about her being milky white and straitlaced. As she's leaving, the table full of china catches her eye with its large number of cups and saucers. A young woman around twenty stands behind the table, smiling shyly, her long blond hair pulled back, her eyes nervously darting. There is something familiar about her, but Natha can't peg it.

"Quite a few cups and saucers you have here," she says to the young woman.

"You can get two for ten dollars. They're antique," she adds.

Natha is immediately drawn to a white cup with bright red bands around it and small gold hearts.

"This one looks like it was for Valentine's Day."

"That one has a hairline crack in the handle," the young woman tells her.

"I'll take it anyway," Natha says. There's something about it. "And this one too," pointing to one with broad orange bands and yellow daisies. She and Ruthie can have coffee in them.

Cups and Saucers.

Christ, she thinks. She's never equated love with china before, now she can't help but think of Jack Callaberry and his lover, Christina, and John Gulliver standing at some farm before the auction, waiting to tell her about the notes they passed between them.

Virginia Woolf said these things just come with an image, the idea for a story, like the fin she saw in the water before she thought of *The Waves*.

Natha hesitates to start writing it in her head. Shit, she thinks, what could have been different about Jack and Christina?

"Why don't you have a lover?" Ruthie once asked her. "If Devon can have them, why can't you?"

"I can," she told Ruthie. "I've just chosen not to. What would be any different with someone else?"

It is better to live with the question than to find the answer, she decides, walking on towards Ruthie's apartment building, especially if there isn't any difference at all. Maybe Jack and Christina's story is unique to John Gulliver, but Natha has surely heard it before countless times. Just not the suicide part. The men she secs don't die from love, they ejaculate it and move on, go home.

Ruthie doesn't answer the door at the first knock, or the second. Natha searches her keys for the right one, finds it, unlocks the door, and enters the apartment to find the day's light shut out by the still-drawn dark-brown curtains. She opens them to see a bottle of rye on the coffee table and a half-filled glass.

"Ruthie," she calls out, then hears the flush of the toilet. She sets the frames and the bag with the teacups on the couch.

"Oh, love, you're here," Ruthie says, coming down the hall, her right arm in a sling.

"Devon left a note for me. I didn't see it until the middle of the night. What did you do?"

"I was dancing and I fell," she says, sitting on the couch, reaching for the bottle.

"You don't need that," Natha tells her.

"Oh, but I do. The pain is awful."

"You already have some in the glass," Natha says.

"Right. Right. Don't suppose you want to join me?"

"Didn't they give you anything for the pain?"

"They won't kick in for a bit. In the meantime, there's this," she says holding up her glass.

"Dancing, were you?"

"I haven't danced in years. What is all this stuff?"

"Frames for your pictures. I'm going to print them later." Natha holds one up.

"For the golden girl," she says.

"They're lovely. I love that they're old and gold."

"I stopped at a yard sale on the way. Look. I got some cups and saucers for our coffee."

"The one with hearts has to be yours."

"Where were you dancing when you fell?"

"Here. In this room. The Rolling Stones."

"By yourself?"

"Yes. I can't even wash my hair now. Look at this mess," she says running a hand through it.

"I'll wash it. Put that down and come into the kitchen."

"Can you get the shampoo in the bathroom and a towel?"

Natha moves a dining chair to the kitchen sink and clears out the pile of dishes.

"My whole gait feels off. I can't walk in a straight line."

She looks concerned.

"You'll be all right, Ruthie. Let me wash your hair and you'll feel better."

Natha grabs the shampoo and a towel from the bathroom.

"Maybe you can work at the library. Fill in while I'm off. My left hip hurts like hell."

"Me? At the library?"

"Something different for you to do. Less of the other."

"I don't even have a social insurance number."

Natha guides Ruthie's head back over the sink and under the warm water as if she were washing a baby's head, caressing gently while Ruthie's hazel eyes search Natha out. How vulnerable, Natha thinks. To be holding another's head under a tap, how violent you could make it, or how loving. She leans over and kisses Ruthie's cheek as she massages in the shampoo.

"I'm not trying to sound like a mother, mentioning the job," Ruthie says. "Wanting something more for you."

"You don't sound like any mother I know, certainly not Irene," Natha quips.

"She's sick," Ruthie says.

"It's you I'm concerned about, Ruthie. Now hush. Let me rinse the shampoo out."

The rush of the water and the smell of the shampoo triggers something in Natha and she feels it in her body, something cold and disturbing; she's done this before, for someone else, someone from long ago. She takes a deep breath and convinces herself she's probably just thinking of when she washes Celia's hair, but the feeling lingers, even as she washes the cups and saucers and makes coffee and sits down with Ruthie to drink it and tells her about John Gulliver and Jack Callaberry and Christina.

"It's just too fucking cute, you know, how they called each other 'Cup' and 'Saucer.' I just don't even believe it."

"You've been at your job too long, love."

"Seriously — you don't find that a little saccharine?"

"Why's John telling you all of this?"

"I must have a sign on my ass. *Men's Confessional*."

A tiny metal sculpture sitting on a shelf catches her eye. A naked woman lying down, defeated. She has seen it before, countless times. *Fallen Woman*, she remembers its name. Today she can hardly take her eyes off it.

"Maybe he likes you," Ruthie says, breaking Natha's fixation on the sculpture.

"Who?" she asks, forgetting the gist of the conversation.

"John Gulliver."

"He doesn't have a clue about me," she snaps.

"How's Devon?"

Natha shrugs. "He's Devon."

Ruthie rolls her eyes.

"Jules called again. Wants to pay me just to talk."

"Are you going to?"

"Would you?"

"Talking's not so bad."

"Our roof leaked during the storm. I have a reason to do it."

"Did John Gulliver ask you if you're married?"

"He seemed to know already."

"He seems very nice."

"He's naive."

"Maybe not," Ruthie says, her mischievous grin the first of the morning.

"I wasn't going to tell you anything."

"You can tell me everything."

She stops short of telling Ruthie about the feeling at the kitchen sink just forty minutes ago, with the shampoo and the water, and young Darlene's blond hair rushing by.

"You can't tell anyone about Jack Callaberry and his lover."

"I won't. Who would I tell? It's this John Gulliver I'm thinking of. I just have this feeling about him, about the two of you."

"Don't be ridiculous, Ruthie."

"Seriously — I just have this feeling," Ruthie repeats.

Ruthie always has these feelings, Natha thinks, and she supposes if she herself had lost two breasts to cancer she too might fall prey to fate and mystery and funny feelings.

"Will you consider the library?"

"Christ, Ruthie. Me in the library?"

"You'd be surrounded by books."

"The point is I'd be *surrounded* by people and by walls. I don't think I could take that."

"Just think about it."

"I like to get in and out of things, you know, drop in here and there. Staying in one place for any length of time, I don't know. Doesn't day-in-day-out with the same people bug the hell out of you?"

"Are we talking about me, or about you?"

"How can any of us stand it?"

"You're in a frightful mood, love."

"I'm feeling very restless."

"Restless? You seem anxious."

"I'm tired. I'm not sleeping."

Natha stands up and paces the room. She sees a bunch of change, mostly quarters, on the edge of the bookcase. Money, she thinks. She needs the money.

"You don't have to worry about me. I can get Susan next door to help out," Ruthie reassures her.

"No — I'm doing it," Natha insists. "What do you need from the store?"

"There's food in the fridge."

If she's going to talk to Jules, it may as well be today, she thinks. She can call Devon and tell him she's staying with Ruthie for a while. Or not call him, just go. "Fucking roof," she swears quietly. All she has to do is talk to him. A thousand bucks.

"What are you thinking, love?"

"I need you to lie for me, if Devon should call here in the next while. I'm going to Jules's, get it over with."

"Now?"

"If Devon calls, just say I went to the store. I won't be that long. Can you do that? Help me out?"

"Of course, love, but —"

"It's no big deal. Don't worry," she says, trying to stiffen her back on the way out, catching one last glance at the tiny sculpture of the fallen woman on the shelf. *Go now*, she hears, *a fallen woman is a poor woman without a cent to her name.*

SHE WALKS WITH SOME urgency past the liquor store and Foodland towards Front Street, hardly feeling her body, just her feet that seem to be taking her in a direction she's not entirely sure she wants to be headed. Her mind is heavy; whose voice was it she heard in Ruthie's apartment, about the fallen woman being poor — a woman's voice, not her own. When she sees the bank at the corner, Virginia Woolf comes to mind. Virginia said a woman needs money and a room of one's own. For fiction, Natha reminds herself — money and a room to write — and she wishes now that she were simply writing this as a scene, not living it, not passing by the bank thinking of how much she'll be able to deposit after this visit with Jules, and how quickly it will go — the cost to herself. She'd rather be at John Gulliver's auction sale hearing a story about love, even if it is a story she can't believe.

"Fuck," she swears as she moves ahead.

The town's too quiet, the sun's light too bright, for her loud, dark, racing thoughts of returning. She will not be defeated by them. She carries on, taking in the sights of Henry Street, a street she has avoided for years, noting that the sidewalk on the right side is still too narrow and crumbly in spots. She could say the same of her life right now — narrow and crumbly, or crumbling, or so it seems, so it feels, this agitation she carries with her past newly renovated apartments in a building that was once a bar, and before that a restaurant, and before that a laundromat, and before that she can't remember — this morphing building she could see from the corner of Henry and Front, catching it out of the corner of her eye on the way to library or the hardware store or The Chocolate Shoppe. Now she is on the forbidden Henry Street, walking past the evolving building, thinking how little her life has changed over the years, still spreading wide for the cocks of those willing to pay, still swimming in the same lake, watching Irene piss herself, still making life easy for Devon.

She walks on, past a piece of empty land where the old arena stood, a half-circle tin structure. She never skated there, preferring the risk of the ice on the Mill Pond and its large expanse, where she could avoid others. She was only in the old arena a few times, at hockey games with Daddy.

Whiskey. Pucks. Fights.

The cold arena air.

She heard that they tore the arena down, but never came by to see it for herself. Even that curiosity wouldn't make her walk along Jules's street again. The long stretch before her to the top of the hill where Jules's house sits is almost too much. Too much time to think and change her mind. Too much time to remember that he spit in his hands and smeared his penis before entering her, shoving himself between her legs saying "Ah. There. Home again." That word *home* fucked her up every time, more than the sex. As if he wasn't trespassing, as if she was his house of gratification.

Natha crosses the street to the left side to pull herself back to the task in mind. The sidewalk is more solid on this side and there is open space, a few acres of grass, a baseball diamond, a tennis court. If she were writing this scene instead of living it she'd call this Games Street, not Henry Street, for more reason than one.

Sylvia and Anaïs and Virginia would approve; especially Plath, she thinks, the tall grasses in the gutter swaying *yes* as a wind from the west suddenly joins the bright light of the day, reminding her that things can change in an instant. She no longer feels fifteen and invaded. She is filling out, feeling her broader hips and full breasts and strong legs, not just her feet. It comes, like inspiration must come, she thinks, like a wind, poking a finger of truth and sharpness into the moment. That's how the creative force must feel, like your body, your mind, suddenly filled with a gust of air that wasn't there before.

As much as she loves the work of Plath and Nin and Woolf, it is their private lives in their journals and diaries that has dug into her skin, making her envious — in particular, how it comes to them, a story, someone else's life, a work of art.

How does a woman tap into that?

She could say she's known inspiration. She just can't remember exactly when it came — the idea to live by her body, by her own rules, plot her own life. It is too easy to say it was just because of Jules. It could have ended with him, but it didn't. Now she's written herself into a corner, ending up here on Henry Street again, looking to Jules for money.

"Let the games begin," she says to herself, remembering how she always wanted to smack a tennis ball, or a baseball — smack something. She can smack Jules, she thinks. Sick and defenceless as he is.

What would Plath have her do? Write about the apprehension she feels as she stands before Jules's house?

She can't seem to steel herself completely.

"Fuck," she says again to the air between herself on the sidewalk and the house before her.

One-ninety-one Henry. It looks smaller. Smaller than all the other houses on the street, a visual trick of some kind played by her mind. Smaller and fake, a toy house set down just to throw her off. The front door is still red and the same heavy, steel-blue curtains hang in the living room window, pulled back, as always. The mailbox outside the front door has been changed. It used to be black, now it is brass. A thousand bills have been delivered since she was last here. Lights shone, water ran, thousands of hours of television flickered blue light at night. The utilities of the past twenty years no doubt paid on time, in full. Jules was an organized bastard, always forthcoming with the money for services rendered.

She has no doubt he'll pay her today.

She walks up the steps and rings the bell with her middle finger — *fuck you* — and waits for a thousand dollars to answer the door.

So this is where life has led her.

In the time she stands there waiting for Jules to answer, she can feel twenty years of hands fingering and pinching her, the dismissive denial of her mother, and the manipulative line Devon walks between granting her freedom and leaning on her to take care of everything. A new truck. Roof repairs. She can feel the lightness of Celia's innocence and the heaviness of the lie of night school. Her inchoate feelings and revulsion of Buddy Francis and the dark something that lies behind the young blond Darlene rushing past her. What is on the other side when the blond hair flashes by?

She is afraid to know.

Even the woman from the 1930s sitting at the rolltop desk accompanies her today. Natha struggles to feel integrity in her decision, this standing here, this convincing herself she is being smart to come here, to talk for a thousand dollars.

She rings the bell again and what she begins to feel is the raw skin of the loss of Daddy when she was fifteen, feeling that she may as well do what Jules asks, Daddy wasn't coming back, there wasn't anyone who was going to come and rescue her.

Maybe that's when the inspiration came — the idea of it — to live by her body, call her own shots, to make transactions to survive — to have the things she needs.

To have things.

Like everyone else.

If she hadn't run into him at Stedman's, with a spatula in his hand, she'd be shocked by the shrunken man who answers the door.

"Well," he says with laboured breath. "Come in, Natha."

Die she wants to say to him. *Will you hurry up and die*, thinking how her life might change if she were to walk through the cemetery and shine her flashlight on his respectable stone, the fine upstanding citizen, the proprietor of the first bookstore, the only bookstore, where the lives of the likes of Plath and Nin and Woolf came to this town.

"I don't like to drink alone much anymore," Jules says, pulling a bottle of cognac out from the bar in the dining room. He sets it on the table and struggles with getting glasses out of the hutch, the ting of them hitting each other goes off like a bell for a wrestling match in her mind. She sits on a wingback chair in the living room, watching him. She'll be damned if she's going to help.

She can smell the mustiness of the place from all of the old furniture in the room — heirlooms passed down from his mother's side of the family, if she remembers correctly. Stately furniture that always seemed out of place in this basic house. She smells the mustiness and the lemon polish on the coffee table in front of her. This house never did feel clean.

Who cleans it now?

The outlet under the television is where she used to plug the vacuum cord when she ran the vacuum over the green carpet. It was an awkward place to plug in, but it was the only one available. The other was behind the walnut bookcases that line the room. She can see Plath's *The Bell Jar* clearly sitting on the same second shelf; beside it, the fat, black cover of her journals. Her own fingerprints and those of Jules stained into the pages.

What's the real reason for his desire to talk, to see her again?

The skin between his legs can no longer stand erect on its own or by his will. Jules: a wounded, dying soldier not likely to be remembered for long by most in this town, not known for any gallantry, and she the one he left an indelible mark on.

What will happen to all of his stuff — the books, the Royal Doulton figurines, the spatula he bought at Stedman's?

He sets the glasses down on the coffee table then settles into a corner of the couch, the same mauve couch that was here before, greying and fading now. It was purchased in the last year of his wife's life. He sips his cognac, never mind that it's still morning; he's dying, he has every right. He sips and looks up and down her bare legs.

"You still look great in shorts," he says.

She pretends to join him, lets her lips touch the liquid fire but doesn't swallow. She only accepted one on the grounds this just might move things along quicker. Get him feeling good, get it over with, the objects in the room stealing her attention, throwing her back. She doesn't want to feel fifteen again, but the curio cabinet with the Royal Doulton girls in their pinafores keep her glued to the girl she once was, the one who thought the age of innocence only existed in make-believe china faces. There certainly was no age of that in Ray and Irene Cole's house.

She tries to find her voice, to make conversation, but a framed black-and-white photograph of wooden stairs in the outdoors leading up to nowhere in particular catches her eye. It wasn't here before.

Climb, she hears in the same woman's voice as before, a strong, confident voice urging her to do something. Climb up, or out? she wonders, circling the rim of her glass with her finger. This is crazy, she thinks.

"What do you think of me dying?" he asks, his eyes searching for something in hers. His eyes remind her of a particular kind of sky — blue but on the verge of white, and soft. Too soft for the forceful man she once knew.

"What about chemo or radiation?" she asks him.

He shakes his head. His breathing is laboured.

"Didn't do any good. I left things too long," he says. "A nurse comes in regularly now."

Silence falls between them.

"So many years ago," he says, wistfully. "It's funny how you can live in the same small town and hardly ever run into each other," he adds.

Luck, she thinks. She's not going to tell him she has seen him, spotted him in the liquor store or Foodland and went out of her way to avoid him.

"Timing," she says in response.

"Yes. Timing," he repeats, letting his eyes take in all of her. "I heard you were married a long time ago. Tell me, what's your husband like?"

She thinks about how to answer that. Of course, he's going to ask.

"Independent," she lies.

"Independent," Jules repeats. "And your daughter? What's her name?"

"You don't need to know that," she answers with a sharpness that seems to catch him off guard. He shifts in his seat and takes a long swallow of his drink.

"Okay, Natha," he says. "Fair enough. But I suppose she's the reason you're here. Her future and all that."

"Suppose all you want."

"I suppose you gave it up years ago — selling yourself, I mean."

This time she lets herself swallow some of her drink. Why wouldn't he think she quit a long time ago? She'll be damned, too, if she'll tell him she never did, that she's still doing it.

How has she let twenty years go by? How does anyone let twenty years go by doing the same thing, like the women in the bank and the man at the hardware store? You start off thinking it'll do for now and before you know it you've been doing the same thing for a couple of decades. Because you do. Because it just happens.

"I heard your father never came back," he says.

"Where did you hear that?"

"Small town," he says. "I was in business here for years. I know a lot of people. And your mother frequents the Legion."

"I guess you pretty much know everything then, don't you, Jules?"

"Tell me how you feel about me dying," he says again.

"You know the meter's ticking, that you have to pay me

today just for having this conversation, so why don't you be specific about what you want?" she tells him.

She is growing impatient with her surroundings; that she's still sitting here in this living room, which hasn't changed one bit. From her seat she sees the hallway leading to the bedrooms. This is like a trap, she thinks, being stuck here as if it were twenty years ago, sitting here with him playing cat-and-mouse and taking forever to get to the point. Jules was always good at deflecting.

More annoying than anything, though, sitting here next to the bookcases, are the memories of the peacefulness she felt when, in the midst of cleaning his house, she'd stop, sit down, and read, the stately antique furniture surrounding her. She could have been anywhere. It felt far away from home, buried as she was in other lives.

Now she sits in her own life waiting to get his sexual wish list. She runs her eyes across the shelves in the bookcase until she finds it — *Lolita*, the book he was holding that day when she was fifteen, telling her he wanted to have sex with her, while she was dusting his dresser, telling her to open the top drawer, finding the box of condoms.

She can hear it now — the sound of a fly buzzing, bouncing off the lamp shade around the heat of the light bulb. Every time it hit the shade she could feel Jules push inside of her until she became the fly and flew away from the heat of the bulb and out of the lampshade and out of the house and across the town back to her own bedroom.

She remembers that now. The fly. How she became the fly in her own mind while he fucked her, while she bled a little from the tear of innocence, while his wife's picture stared out at her.

"You never told me what your wife died of," she says. He never said much about his wife, Audrey, at all.

"A weak heart. I woke up one morning and she was dead in bed beside me. I wish my own death could be like that. Tell me how you feel about me dying, Natha."

"Did you love her?

Jules stares into her eyes. She doubts he loved anyone. She stares back to defy him to answer.

"That's not what we were supposed to talk about today," he says.

"Did you love anyone, ever?" He leans forward, runs a hand along the polished coffee table.

"Tell me," he says, "in all your experience, all these years of clients and from your own marriage, tell me what you know about love, Natha."

She doesn't say anything.

"What do you want from me, Jules?"

He leans back into the corner of the couch. She can see he is tired now.

"I keep thinking that by some miracle I'll be able to do it again. That you will be that miracle, Natha."

As if it's possible, she thinks.

"If anyone can, you can," he adds. "And even if nothing happens, I'll get to spend some time with you. So, you'll do it?"

"Not now," she answers.

"When?"

"It's more like *if*," she answers coldly. She looks towards the bookcase once again.

"You can have the books, if you want," he says.

"I have my own copies," she says.

"I loved watching you read, Natha. When you took a break from the housework and curled up with Sylvia Plath. The times I did see you."

"I mostly read when you weren't here."

"I know," he says. "I know. There's a kind of necessary intercourse between life and literature, wouldn't you say? One doesn't come without the other."

"I'm not here for your take on books and life, Jules."

"I never interrupted your reading."

"You interrupted my life."

"I loved you," he says.

"Like hell you did."

"I did. Because of your plight."

"My plight?"

"Your father taking off like that. Your mother — the mess she was and you quitting school to clean houses. It was like … it was something right out of a book."

He stands up shakily and walks to his desk.

"I'll write a cheque now for a thousand so you know I mean business," he says. "I think you'll know what to do to make the miracle happen and I will pay twenty times this just for trying."

He sits down and painstakingly fills out a cheque. The silence that settles in the house is almost unbearable. She can hear him wheezing. She assumes the cancer has spread. Of course he left it too long. A man like him so attached to his cock would be humiliated that it doesn't work anymore. She wonders who he tried to fuck and couldn't, or did he just lie on this greying, faded couch and try to get himself off.

Christ, she thinks, can I really do this again, even for all the money in the world?

"You know," he says, turning away from the desk, almost falling over. "I used to hate how you would run off right after. I always wanted you to stay for dinner. You know, talk about the books."

He hands her the cheque and she looks to make sure it's filled out properly.

"Goddammit, Natha. I can still write a cheque."

She stands up and meets him eye-to-eye.

"You were born with the wrong eyes," she tells him. "They're too soft for a man like you."

"The clincher in this deal is that you have to tell me what you know about love, and what you think about me dying."

"I'll have to think about that. About everything," she says, heading to the door. She can feel him trying to catch up to her, but she darts down the front steps.

"And I want the truth," he shouts, just before she hits the sidewalk.

IT IS HER THIRTY-FIVE-YEAR-OLD self that accompanies Celia to the park in the afternoon — "The Me House Park," as Celia calls it. The two of them sit inside a small playhouse, Natha watching Celia sifting a handful of sand on the window ledge, methodically removing tiny stones and twigs so the sand piles cleanly into a round shape. It's *your* house, Natha told her when she was only three. Celia wouldn't say *my* house, only *me* house.

"It's going to be a pie, Mommy. A chocolate pie."

Natha holds it together, suggesting stones for raisins and twigs for cinnamon sticks. She helps Celia arrange them on the sand pie.

"Will it be here when we come back next time?" Celia asks.

Natha doesn't want to tell her not likely.

"What if it isn't, my sweet girl? What if some other children come and make something else out of the pie?"

Celia shrugs.

"I guess that's okay, Mommy. Then we can make something else again."

Make something else.

The words ride piggyback on the rest of Natha's day, more of a command than a thought, in her own determined voice. She arrives at Ruthie's in time to make dinner, having corralled Devon into ordering pizza for Celia and himself, despite his plans to go to Barb's again. Later, she tells him, she won't be gone long.

"YOU'RE IN AN AWFULLY good mood for where you went today," Ruthie remarks while Natha prepares a cheese and mushroom omelette. "I thought you'd be a mess tonight."

They manoeuvre around each other in the small, cramped kitchen.

"He wants to know what I know about love," she tells Ruthie.

"What for?

"He also wants to know how I feel about him dying."

"My God, love, he wants you to care," Ruthie says.

"He thinks I'm going to be cynical about love," Natha tells her. "But I'm going to surprise him. I'm going to make something out of it, out of love."

"What on earth are you talking about?"

"I'm going to call John Gulliver and I'm going to hear this love story about Jack and Christina — Cup and Saucer — and whatever I find out, I'm going to make it my own and tell Jules about it."

"What about sex? Does he want you to have sex with him? How can he even have sex?"

"That's the least of my worries, Ruthie. I need something more to make him write that cheque."

"Like love?"

"Yes, like love."

"You really want his money?"

"I want choice in my life right now. Money is the freedom to choose."

"Choose what?"

Natha flips the omelette.

"Christ," she says. "I don't know yet. But the sex won't be enough. It may not even have to happen if I find out something really good about love."

"And this will put you where?" Ruthie asks with some frustration.

"It puts me in control."

Ruthie puts her head in her hand.

"This is all very sad to me," she says. "That you have to look somewhere else for that kind of story."

"That bastard was always philosophically circling me when I was young, throwing big questions out to me I didn't know how to answer."

"What kind of questions?"

"'Does a man have to be present in your life for you to know he carries your life around with him?' Fuck, I'm just remembering that now."

"Was he talking about himself or your father?"

"I never knew. I just remember the confusion I felt. This time I'm going to nail the answer."

"And John Gulliver?"

"He wants to tell me the story anyway, so it's win-win. I'm just doing what writers do — borrowing someone else's story."

"But won't Jules know that story, about Jack?"

"I can change it to make it my own. Shit, I don't know. Maybe I'll just tell him Jack's story. I wonder, at what point does a writer decide such a thing?"

"I don't know, love. I have this feeling," Ruthie says.

She wants to snap back at Ruthie, for not being positive about this, but bites her tongue, seeing the sling around her shoulder, and her looking tired from the pain.

"I know you do," she tells her. "Just trust me on this."

Natha serves the omelette along with salad.

Over dinner, Ruthie asks, "Do you care about Jules dying?"

"Why would I?" Natha responds.

"Does it bother you?"

"It stirs things up. That's all."

"If I had the money to give, so help me, you wouldn't have to think about this. Is it really worth it?"

"Trust me," Natha tells her again. "Just trust me."

"TRUST ME," JOHN GULLIVER says to her over the phone later at night, while Devon is reading Celia a bedtime story and she is alone at her desk in the living room. "It's a true story."

"I was thinking," she says, "Can we meet somewhere instead of me coming early to another auction?"

"That'll be difficult. This is the busy season in my world."

"You don't have a day off?"

"Sunday, but I have to be here, with Mary. By the way, this is the time of day when I'm in my office alone returning the day's phone calls. It's the only good time to call me, or else she'd be really annoyed about this."

"I understand. So, you work every day?

"If I don't have a sale, I have listings. That's when I go to the homes and list all the items — after I've heard their whole goddamn life story."

"Right," she says. "I didn't think of that."

"There's the listing and the life story. Then on the day of sale, I show up with two other guys who work for me and we haul all their shit out, which I've already told them they won't get what they thought they would for it. Then I'm a goddamn windup toy on that box, selling the stuff."

"But you're good at it," she says.

"Let me see," he says. "I've got some time tomorrow

morning between nine-thirty and eleven and I'll be out your way anyway. Where do you want to meet?"

She thinks quickly. Devon will be home tomorrow, so not here. She doesn't want to meet in some restaurant. Then it dawns on her that the small parkette at King's Mill is not so far away.

"King's Mill," she says. "The park there. At a picnic table."

"Nine-thirty," he repeats. "I'm glad you called," he continues. "I actually missed you out at the auction today."

"I had a friend in need," she says.

"I hope you'll be able to call me a friend someday," he says.

RUTHIE'S HEAD AND SHOULDERS come out of the printer first.

Natha happens to glance at the date on the screen. Monday now, June twenty-third. 1:05 a.m.

She reaches into her desk for a pen to write the date on the back of the print and finds the *God favours the brave* card with the woman standing in line at the falafel stand in Bangkok. She can use this now, she thinks, and sets it on the desk. She has already placed sea-green mats she had hanging around the house on the desk to help offset the photographs in the gold frames, which she brought home from Ruthie's after dinner. When she picked them up from Ruthie's coffee table, she caught sight of the sculpture of the fallen woman again. *Get up*, commanded the same woman's voice she heard before.

Ruthie's breastless chest and her vagina come out next, her arms hanging at her sides. Now she has a broken shoulder.

Natha moves a couple of frames over to one side of the

desk so she has room to start framing Ruthie's head and shoulders. There's a sudden noise, like something has dropped to the floor. She looks around the side of the desk and sees Celia's small silver princess crown.

For all of your crowning achievements.

This really is crazy, she thinks, this voice out of nowhere. She can't think of a time when this has happened before. It would be amusing if it didn't feel so real. She shrugs it off. It's stress, this sudden running commentary.

Christ, she's just tired. Up too early. The yard sale. Concern for Ruthie. The long, anxious walk to Jules's.

She checks her email to see if Dr. David Riddell has replied — nothing. She is happy with the look of the sea-green mat against Ruthie's body parts in the forest. She watches the pixels fill in Ruthie's feet, then her shins and kneecaps, and they don't seem like they belong to anyone real. The feet, the legs that danced and tripped.

Maybe all of this is what she felt a week ago, in the early days of June, the early-on of something — Ruthie getting hurt, running into Jules, talking to John Gulliver.

She knows she felt something then.

Now she feels worn out from the sudden increased speed of life.

That Piper man's still-ticking pocket watch goes off in her mind.

Like his Christmas decorations.

And his coffee mugs.

She finishes framing the prints.

She may not know much about love, but she can say life

is about body parts and objects. Aluminum trays and antique medicine cabinets and Jules's little girl Royal Doulton figurines swing their pinafores as she turns off the desk lamp and heads upstairs for bed.

It doesn't seem that long ago that her days were routine and uneventful to her and there was little to think about. Now her head is full of thoughts. She lays her head on the pillow. It is clear to her that life has a calendar of its own and it is useless to believe that a particular day in June one year will be the same on that particular day the next year, even when the clock beside your bed never changes. It is the same small, black, digital clock she's had for the last ten years with its forever-moving red numbers that only end up in the same place at the same time on any given day.

TEN

NATHA STANDS IN A small park area with a clear view of
the second floor of King's Mill. Squire Creek flows westward, much slower now than the early spring rush, carrying
the possibility that it was something else that made Jack
Callaberry hang himself, not love. Could it not have been the
routine of the auction life? She'd like to ask John Gulliver if it
doesn't make him desperate, selling people's stuff, and having
to hear their life stories. She'd like to tell him she understands
that part of it. When she thinks about all the stories she's
heard herself within the four walls of a motel room, it's
enough to make her in need of a different kind of story altogether. Isn't that why she's here? For her own sake, and yes,
for something moving enough to satisfy Jules's curiosity about
what she knows about love.

The red-winged blackbirds that grace the marsh to the
right pierce her thoughts. The peacefulness of the place is what
she wants to take in right now, the lack of wind, the smell
of dust from the road as it heightens and settles when a car

speeds by. It is not a dirty smell in her mind and reminds her of the dirt roads she travelled on with Daddy all those years ago, on the way to the farm to bring in hay. How it mixed with the smell of the fresh-cut fields and Daddy's ease of being with her. He never showed any signs of awkwardness with his daughter and it seemed he wanted to know she shared his opinions and views, as if everything had to pass her judgment, and to know everything was always okay.

"Everything all right by you?" he'd ask, running a thumb softly down the side of her cheek.

He'd be sixty-three now, not as old as Jules. "No," she'd like to say to him. "Everything's not all right."

She sits down at one of the picnic tables and lights a cigarette. On the first exhale, John Gulliver pulls up in his black truck. The sun's glare on the windshield prevents her from seeing him clearly. It is not until he steps out of the truck, carrying two coffees, that she can see he is in a serious mood, though he smiles slightly at the sight of her.

Ruthie once said that she believes when two people have sex, something of their souls transfers from one to another. Natha watches John make his way over and wonders if the same thing happens to him when he's standing in people's houses, listening to their life stories, brushing up against the walls of their homes. Does something of their souls get transferred onto his muscular shoulders? If that's the case, she thinks, their meeting here today will ride on the will of a thousand souls, not just the two of them.

"I don't know how you take it," he says, setting cream and sugar in front of her, handing her one of the coffees.

He sits down next to her on the picnic table, not across from her, and wipes his brow.

"So, here we are," he sighs.

"The scene of the crime," she says.

"This is actually where a lot of things took place, Natha."

He looks straight at her with his thinking, seeking eyes.

"You look tired," he says. "Are you all right?"

"I'm fine," she tells him.

"And your friend in need — is she or he all right?"

"She'll be fine. Broke a shoulder."

"Ouch," he says. "I guess that's a good reason for you not coming to the sale on Saturday."

"It's good enough in your books, is it?"

"I was hoping it wasn't anything I said or did. Of course, I was wondering."

"Nothing to do with you at all," she reassures him. "Thanks for the coffee."

"They used to meet here sometimes — Jack and Christina. She lived just up the road."

"I know."

"Before this was officially a park area, they used to meet here when her husband was at work."

"Jack told you that?"

"He told me everything. Showed me all the notes they passed between them at the auctions. She gave him her notes from him when she ended the relationship and he had kept all of hers."

"Do you still have them?"

"Burned them a long time ago. But they're still all up

here," he says, pointing to his temple.

"You remember them?"

"I can see them in my mind."

"How many were there?"

"A lot."

"What do you mean you see them?"

"Photographic memory. The same way I remember people who haven't come to my auctions in years. I remember their faces and their names and what they bought. It's just the way my mind works. It's visual."

"You do have a good memory. I know that," she says.

"More than you can imagine," he tells her. "I know it sounds crazy, but —"

He shrugs his shoulders and swallows some coffee.

"I wish I didn't," he says quietly and looks out towards the distant marshland.

It hits her now. That this is the first time she has sat with a man who isn't waiting for some kind of sex to begin. An honest man with too much kept inside. All the bravado of John Gulliver the auctioneer has no place here. Now he is just a man with the burden of a story. No doubt a story that has shaped his own life, no matter how unintentionally.

In the sun, in this hour, something is seeded, between the watched and the watcher. Natha can't help but feel for him as she watches him watch the red-winged blackbirds flitting about, trying to decide where to start. At least, that's what she thinks he is thinking about and she is willing to give him all the time in the world to decide when to start, as if she herself has just been given an abundance of patience. Maybe it's the outdoors, she thinks, the open freedom of this place instead of the four walls of a motel and some guy who just wants to fuck her. Patience is in the oak and ash trees swaying in the breeze, in the sound of the creek meandering its way past them. Mostly, though, she feels this patience inside of herself, a kind of calm she hasn't known before, not like this, not with a man, not even Devon.

When John looks back at her, his eyes look sore and tired and bottled up — eyes that could cry for a long time if he let them. She feels an urge to stroke his face, to trace her finger under his eyes with the softest touch so he might feel the unexpectedness of it, the rarity of such a compassionate gesture on her part. She refrains, though, reminding herself that this is not what this meeting is about. Still, his eyes ask to be known, to be understood.

"What?" she asks him. "What is it?"

"I actually missed you on Saturday," he says. "I don't know what it is, but the day just wasn't right. I thought you were coming and when you didn't, it's like the air went out of me and it wasn't my best sale. That's how Jack felt whenever Christina didn't show up at a sale. That's what he said — that the air went out of him."

No longer able to look him in the eye, she reaches into her bag for another cigarette.

"Would you like one?" she asks just to break the conversation.

"I haven't had a cigarette in years. Sure," he says.

She lights one for him and then one for herself and gazes back at the marshland.

"Jack was the salt of the earth," John says, exhaling. "People expected things of him, then he goes and falls in love with another woman — a married woman, to boot."

"It happens," she tells him. "All the time."

John stretches his feet out and crosses them, smoking his cigarette slowly as if he is meditating on it.

"'Tell me,' Jack said. 'Do my eyes reveal me out there? No matter how hard I try to focus on the bidders, it is your face I return to, and I am thankful when you raise your hand on a cup and saucer just for the chance to look at you directly for more than a second.'"

"That was in one of the notes?" Natha asks.

"Yes. From early on. "

"That's an old story," she says. "Everyone's still living that one out."

"So, what's the point?" he demands. "That it isn't important?"

"You're intense, John."

He stands up and then in front of her.

"I want to be real with you," he says. "I want real, and I want honest. I want to talk to you about it. I *need* to talk to you about it."

"I thought that's what we were doing."

"Just don't fling it off. Like it didn't matter. Love matters, Natha."

He walks a few steps away to the edge of the park area, closer to the creek. Who is this man? she wonders. It's strange to be in his presence without a crowd surrounding him, a bare man, standing alone, without the crowded lawn of antiques and dishes and cups and saucers. You don't really see a man until he's standing alone at the water's edge with nothing but himself to consider — where he stands in this land when money and possession have no place in the scenario. He rubs his forehead and she can't help but think of the explosion of images and words that crowd his mind, vying for seconds of his time. That one story has been playing itself over and over again for so many years. She sees it now — the importance of him telling her the story just to get it out, get it off his mind, release it. Why he's chosen to tell her still isn't all that clear. Then again, why wouldn't he choose her, standing on the edge of his sales as she does? A loner. Obviously not in with the crowd.

Of course he would pick her.

"Will you walk with me?" he says as he turns around back towards her.

"Sure," she says. "Are you all right?"

"You make me all right," he tells her. "Do me a favour. Don't do anything that makes me fall for you."

"You're crazy," she says, jokingly, as she stands up and starts walking beside him. She could pull him down right now, down to the grass, make him come, release him. There's a part of her that wants just to soothe him and to show him she can make him fall for her. She could do it — lay him down and fuck him and walk away like nothing had happened, but she isn't so sure he could. She's sure he couldn't. Besides, a greater part of her doesn't want that. A greater part of her likes that he is walking by her side, unlike Devon, who wouldn't yesterday — Sunday — when her day was filled with Jules's question — What do you know about love? — and she actually asked Devon to walk down the old railway line with her while Celia was playing at Amy's for a few hours. "That's your thing," Devon said.

Now John chooses a slow pace, asks for another cigarette.

"Smoking this makes me feel rebellious," he says.

"Like a bad boy," she teases him.

"I have to be in such control," he tells her. "This cigarette is my *fuck it*."

"I'd say that's a restrained *fuck it*, John."

He laughs.

"It's the best I can do for now," he says, stopping to light it.

She walks on, reaching the curve in the road, patience once again filling her mind and body, passing the dusty tall grass alongside, the mill just around the corner. It's not long before he's back by her side and their footsteps fall into sync, their shoes kicking the odd stone on the hardened dirt road. They walk without speaking. How long? How long has this road been here? How long the old, split-rail fences and the trees that tower above? All this winds its way through her mind. Mostly, though, she wonders how long it is since she walked with a man. The only place Devon walks is to the Me House Park with Celia, or to Front Street for the Santa Claus Parade in early December. She only asked him Sunday because the walls were closing in and he seemed to follow her from room to room. She wanted to take it outside. She even contemplated telling Devon that she would be meeting John on Monday then dismissed it as too complicated. She doesn't want him to know about the love story between Jack and Christina, or about Jules and the money. If anything, she would have told him just to get him going — that she is spending time with another man and that it doesn't have anything to do with fucking for money. Which reminds her now — Stephen, her client the lawyer, called yesterday and sheis to meet him at the Sunrise tonight at eight. She'll be stuck between four walls soon enough. Shit, she thinks. Enjoy this walk.

The road. The trees. The birds.

John.

The synchronicity of their feet echoes loudly in her ears, and the knowledge that she'll remember this walk always surges through her. The future memory, the present calm. The bridge now, with the rush and the trickle on either side.

"Did Jack die in the spring? I can't remember," she says.

"It was June," John answers. "Like now, only dark and at night."

"I wonder if he heard it."

"Heard what?"

"The creek. The wind in the trees. Everything."

"I've played what that night must have been like for him a thousand times in my mind. If only the door had been locked like it is now. Maybe it wouldn't have happened, but the province didn't take over this site to preserve it until years later."

They stop beside the mill and all she can think about is the second floor and the thick beams.

"That was one note he didn't write," John says.

"Nothing at all?"

"Silence. But I knew something was up when he gave me all the notes between them about a month before — told me everything. He asked me to burn them after I read them. For the longest time I couldn't. It was about a year later that I finally did. Before that I kept them in a box in our barn."

"And you never told your wife about any of it?"

He looks at her with surprise.

"She only knew it as a rumour, like everyone else. She never saw the proof. I made sure of that."

He kicks at a stone on the road.

"Christina lived just up the road," he says. "Come on, I'll show you."

"I know. It's the schoolhouse."

"I feel like walking anyway," he tells her. "Or do you have some place to be?"

"No," Natha says. "I'll walk with you."

There's barely any space between them as they head north along King's Mill Road. She feels the brush of his arm once in a while and she fights the urge to take him into the clover field they pass, this honest man whose only rebellion in life is to smoke someone else's cigarettes. What she could do to him. But the morning sun settles her into complacency, letting him lead the way, as though she's never been led before by anyone and the many layers of sounds on the morning road — the birds, a distant tractor, the wind now picking up and rustling the leaves on the trees — make her feel far away from the night that awaits her, far away from the return of Jules in her life, far away from anything she's been before. Maybe that's why she feels the need to have sex with him, to hold on to something of herself in all of this, while she slips farther down the road, feeling like this will lead somewhere if she just keeps walking.

The sudden halt of his feet jars her. She was only looking down the long and narrow road, losing herself in the moment. Now she sees the red-brick schoolhouse before her, with its white trim and black-shingled roof. No one appears to be home — no car in the driveway, no movement from within.

"Something went on in this schoolhouse," John says. "I'll tell you about it sometime."

"Why not now?"

He turns to look at her.

"It will only shock you, the way you were shocked when I told you my baby died at three weeks. I saw the look on your face, Natha."

She'd almost forgotten. Christ, she thinks, how could I forget that? But it serves no purpose to kick herself over it. Isn't that what we do? Get caught up in the story of the moment, what's in it for me?

"You've got that look now," he says.

"I'm sorry," she says. "That must be so painful."

"He died in the crib."

"A son," she remarks.

"Jack," he says. "She wouldn't try for another one," he adds.

"Christ," Natha says. "I'm so sorry that happened to you."

"It was a long time ago. Time takes care of these things."

"Then why are you still so haunted by Jack Callaberry?"

"I don't know. I just am. It's what was between them."

"Love?"

"Devotion," he says. "You don't find that in this world anymore."

"Did Christina have children?"

"A daughter at the time of the affair. Jack never told me her name and they didn't use any names in their notes. Jack said it was in case they ended up in the wrong hands, like one of them falling on the ground at a sale. They kept each other's notes until the end. It was something they just did."

A few loose hairs blow across her face and John brushes them back, as he did before at that Piper sale on Church Street. Gently, innocently.

"I don't know what it is when you do that," she says.

"What do you mean?"

"You make me feel like I've never been touched before. That's not a come on. It's just a fact."

The words leave her mouth before she can think, but as soon as they're out, she regrets them. He looks at her quizzically, then turns back to look at the schoolhouse. She's not even sure it's true that he makes her feel like she's never been touched before but there was something about it. Maybe it is true and she just can't handle that fact. Christ, she's not going let this swim in her head. She thought it. She said it. It's done.

"I really didn't mean anything by that," she says.

"Nothing taken," he answers, but something in him changes. He seems more relaxed, lets his shoulders drop and smiles at her differently — a trusting smile. "I said I wanted to be honest with you," he tells her. "Christina was the epitome of honest. I bet you keep most of your life to yourself."

Now he is talking again in a low, serious voice and she can see his mouth moving and the words filter in bits and pieces while her body disappears from her and she feels only the weight of her head.

Couldn't leave her husband.

She wanted the romance.

Won't hurt my daughter.

Just love me, Jack.

No promises, no mistakes.

A note from Cup to Saucer.

Natha stands there, listening, but her mind drifts and the ambience of the morning road muffles John's words. Is it worth it, hearing all of this? Jules won't believe it if she tells him this happened to her, this kind of love. She can't make it her own story, or can she? Daddy always said, when you cast out your line to catch a fish, throw it out someplace where you know they're biting.

Daddy said a lot of things.

Daddy, no, I'm not all right.

Washing Ruthie's hair.

Washing hair.

Washing Buddy Francis's daughter Darlene's hair.

A man's naked lap.

That's what she saw when Darlene rushed by and flashed out of the picture.

She feels sick.

"She told him, 'Don't ask me to do anything but love you.'"

Natha hears John now and the birds' song and the wind rustling the trees returns, louder than before.

"I should go," she tells him.

"Okay," he says. "Are you all right?"

"I'm fine," she says. "Can we walk back now?"

"After you," he says, gesturing for her to start walking.

"Can I have another cigarette?" he asks.

She pulls two out from her case and helps him light his, then lights one up for herself. She doesn't know what that was — that fading out. She only knows it felt real — remembering Daddy's words as if he had just said them and washing something out of the young Darlene's hair — the sick feeling.

Walking back, she has no desire to strip John and rest herself on top of him as she did earlier and she wishes she could have heard everything he said when he recited that last note from Cup to Saucer — all the words Christina used. Now she'll have to take the parts she did hear and something from her own life, no matter how foreign all this stuff is, and spin it, making it something tangible for Jules.

Isn't that what writers like Woolf and Plath did?

At least some of it will be true. Christina's words and her own imagined words, whatever they could possibly be, spoken as if she actually said them. Like "You make me feel like I've never been touched before." At least there's some use for them, after all. No matter how unlikely they were to be true

ELEVEN

SHE SITS IN A chair, legs stretched out, her feet on Stephen's lap, smoke from her cigarette hanging in the air between them. He hates that she smokes and she often refrains, at least until the sex is over and done with. Tonight, she thinks of John Gulliver and his rebellion and has decided on a little of her own. Stephen coughs — a fake cough if she's ever heard one. *Fuck him,* is her attitude after the afternoon she's had — the shitty conversation with Devon over where she was this morning. All in all, the patient calm of the morning road at King's Mill has thinned like the smoke in front of her. She puts her cigarette out and takes a sip of Stephen's scotch.

"You're in a bad mood," he says. "Anything you want to talk about?"

She's been seeing him for about three years now, ever since he was divorced, less in the last six months now that he's acquired a serious girlfriend. Trouble is she won't put out until they've reached the one-year mark. He has his needs, he has told her. He may even need her in the future if the sex isn't as good as he'd like it to be. He's a family lawyer, rich and arrogant, and if he only knew what she thought of his sexual skills he'd likely go elsewhere where someone else would croon for his copper. Natha doesn't say anything one way or the other. His money is good and he doesn't need to hear that she loves him. He's too cynical for that. Realistic, he would rather she say.

He slides a hand along her bare leg. She flinches.

"What was that?" he asks, laughing.

"I don't know," she answers.

She doesn't flinch at a man's touch.

He begins to rub her right foot. The cigarette smoke still hangs in the air, adding to the unseen filth of the place. It's in the sheets, the filth. She knows they've been washed, but she's lain on them before, someone's semen stain spotting the bed. The carpet with its collective hairs must surely be at least ten years old by now. The curtains even older, orange and thick from dust and smoke, closed now to ward off the headlights of cars pulling into other rooms. There's only a trace of a television on next door, but it's enough to intrude on the box she is trying to put around herself and Stephen.

If this has to be done, let it not be part of another life. She doesn't want to think of another life, not even if it's a stranger lounging on a bed watching some cop show.

"Trouble in paradise?" Stephen fishes.

He takes his shirt off now, his chest hair sparse and greying early at forty-three.

He picks up her left foot and starts rubbing.

"I've met someone," she tells him. How far could she make the story go?

"Someone?" he asks.

"No one you'd know." She says it but then thinks it is possible he knows John Gulliver, or has heard of him, since he's got a name for himself in the area.

"But what does he know? You know, about you?"

"You're so predictable, Stephen. To even bring that part of it up. Do you think it's all about what we do? Maybe he just likes who I am." She smiles when she says it. He's such a cynic.

"Well, excuse me," he says. "Of course he likes who you are. You mean, you actually let someone know *who* you are? I don't even know that. Who is this guy?"

"He's an honest man. Not like you at all."

"Are you in love?"

"Don't be ridiculous. But I do like him. Is that also what it's all about? Love?"

"You of all people, Natha, should know it's not."

"And what about Julie, your girlfriend? What's that about?"

He thinks for a moment, taking a long gulp of scotch.

"Necessity," he says, setting the glass back down on the table.

"What about love?"

"That too."

"I don't believe you," she says. "Then again, I don't know much about love. What do you know about love, Stephen?"

"You're way too philosophical tonight. Can we just get it on?"

"Seriously — I want your take on it."

She takes her feet away and sits up, grabbing his drink for another sip.

"Okay," he says. "I don't believe it isn't without motive."

"It can't be pure?"

"It's born out of need," he answers, standing up. "It lives out of need and it dies out of need."

He takes his pants off, then his underwear, and stands before her naked with an erection. She has the sudden urge to leave. Her throat is tight and her muscles clenched. Can she actually do this tonight? John Gulliver's gentle stroke, moving her hair out of her face, is the only kind of touch she wants right now. Now with this standing in front of her, the space between her legs is as dry as a bone and unwilling. She can't even think of her vagina. Her skin screams "No." She would suggest just talking tonight, but Stephen would choke on that. So would she. She doesn't want to talk to him, can hardly stand being in the same room with his pushiness and his penis.

Shit.

Fuck.

She's losing her edge.

She stands and takes his hand and leads him to the bed. Thankfully, the television next door has gone silent. She lies down, Stephen falling on top of her, kissing her neck, pulling her hair tight around the top of her head, his feet rubbing up against hers. The skin on her legs chafes with his touch. When he starts to undo her shorts she flinches again.

"Easy," he whispers into her ear, then he bites it, then probes it with his tongue.

If she could only hear the rush and the trickle of Squire Creek at King's Mill and think of the road — the dusty grasses, the rocks piled along the split-rail fencing.

Yes, back there with the birds rising loud in her ears.

The two of them in step with each other.

Walking side by side.

What did he say? *Do me a favour and don't do anything to make me fall for you.*

STOP EXPLAINING IS WHAT she told herself all afternoon when Devon demanded to know why she had to spend time with John Gulliver. She couldn't tell him about the love story or about Jules's question and the money.

"He's just someone I'm spending time with right now," is all she said after she told Devon that just because John's a man doesn't mean it has to be about sex.

"He may as well be a woman," she said. "And I'm learning a lot about antiques."

"I'd rather it be about sex," Devon shouted when they were standing in the kitchen. He slammed a cupboard door and some paint chipped off.

She walked out of the house at that point.

The push inside of her now is dry and raw and, Christ, she can feel herself down there, Stephen between her folds of skin with his cock, stabbing her, really. Ripping the hell out of all other thought. His lawyer chest flattening her own. He feels heavier, panting, moaning in her ear.

With Stephen, she doesn't have to move. He doesn't demand anything but that she lie there, taking him until he comes.

The ceiling looks like it hasn't been painted in decades. Grey and slightly yellow from the table lamp beside her. A spent man still inside her.

What could she possibly do to make John Gulliver fall for her?

Sunday was worse than this tonight. She spent that day at home with Devon. She was anxious after seeing Jules on Saturday, anxious Devon might pick up on it, prod her with questions, but he seemed to be in his own land, smoking joint after joint, passing out on the couch. She played with Celia until it was time for her to go to her friend Amy's. Natha walked home and then wanted to go right back outside.

"Come on," she said to Devon. "Walk with me."

"That's your thing," he said. "I'll stay here."

So she did. Walked alone down the old railway line, her life as she knew it growing more distant as she walked for an hour, way out into the countryside.

When she came home, Devon had a nice roast chicken on the go and didn't say a word about her mood. He came up behind her while she was washing vegetables and rubbed the knot in her back.

"I'm going away Tuesday. Up to Terry's to fish for a few days. Got this guy Gord MacDonald coming to fix the roof. He was guessing a few thousand to do the job. You can write him a cheque."

The house smelled like a home with the chicken in the oven but it felt empty, run by someone no longer there.

"You're good, as usual," Stephen says, rolling over, lying on his back.

She lights a cigarette and lies back herself.

"If there's ever a time I wanted to smoke, it's this time. After the sex, I mean."

"Knock yourself out," she tells him, offering a cigarette.

"Don't be ridiculous, Natha. People die from that shit."

"People die from all kinds of shit," she adds, thinking of Jack Callaberry up there on the second floor of the mill with a rope, just a minute from Christina's schoolhouse.

Something happened there, John had said.

"I wonder what will happen with you and your girlfriend, Stephen."

He springs out of bed, begins to dress.

"Are you in a better mood now?" he asks her.

"Better than what?"

"Whatever was bothering you, does it seem so important now?"

"No, no," she jokes. "Your cock took it all away."

"You'd be a hard person to love, Natha. I wish that new guy of yours good luck. But what about the problem of your husband?"

"I was only joking," she says. "I haven't met anyone. I only told you that to see what you'd say."

"And?"

"You're just too fucking predictable, Stephen. You assume what I do is what I am."

Dressed, he walks towards the door while she continues to lie on the bed finishing her cigarette.

"I don't assume, Natha. I have no idea who you are and it's best that way."

He closes the door quietly behind him.

IT TAKES HER A long time to get out of the bed. All she can smell is Stephen's semen in the condom he left on the bed, and from the Kleenex he wiped himself with and threw onto the floor beside her. It's not a smell she wants to hold on to.

She closes her eyes. She sees John Gulliver standing alone by the creek, before they went for the walk. The lone man. No crowd around him. No furniture and tables behind him. She thought she saw innocence. Worn-out innocence. Perhaps that's been gone ever since Jack Callaberry told John of his love affair. But no, she thinks, it's more than that. Perhaps it's John's feelings about his marriage, about Mary, the wife who so very clearly has never moved past what happened to her father.

Christ, Natha thinks, am I not the same?

Daddy, no, I'm not all right.

The television sound returns and intrudes on her thoughts. She pulls herself up and goes to the bathroom, sees a silverfish scuttling along the baseboard, slipping into a hole.

Dirty bathrooms and silverfish.

If John Gulliver only knew.

She wipes herself and jumps into the shower, lets the water drain this other life off of her.

Think Celia, she tells herself. Sweet child she gave birth to.

She can't wait to get home now, to fall into bed with the one person who —

Stop, she tells herself. She can't put that burden on a small child. Buck up, bear it. She dries herself and gets dressed, drinks the last of Stephen's glass of scotch.

Then there are the stars.

Tonight, a full blast of stars.

She looks at the heavens for the longest time before

getting into her car. She leaves the windows down so that the wind will dry her hair. Tonight the drive home seems to go on forever, like the sex did, Natha pushing herself to endure it. She felt she could fall into a downward spiral if she allowed herself. She may not be the most lovable person, but she sure as hell can endure anything for half an hour — longer if the need be. As long as it doesn't turn into the next day. The next day has to promise something else. She knows a day can make a difference. Celia was born on a next day. Daddy left on a next day. She met John Gulliver on a next day.

All she wants now is the next day.

Her vagina is sore, her head pounding.

On a night like this, there is only the next day to keep you going, even if that going is back home to an empty house.

Celia, she thinks.

Think of Celia.

With horror, she realizes how far from her mind Celia has been.

Christ.

The farms.

The houses.

The lake.

The town.

My little girl's room.

TWELVE

Natha crawls into the bed of the child of her own blood and that fact alone makes her heart stop. Celia, still asleep, knowing it is her mother who lies next to her. *In sleep we trust. It is the waking hours that thrust us into a defensive state.* So Natha thinks, wrapping an arm around her daughter's waist, her shampooed hair reminding Natha that she wasn't there for Celia's bath tonight. She doesn't like that Devon still washes her hair, now that Celia is six. She strokes Celia's hair, kisses her head. Tomorrow she'll change things. She'll not go out anymore until she has bathed Celia.

There's something about the smell of the shampoo that catches her in the throat.

Tomorrow she'll be more attentive to Celia. *Where have I been?* she asks herself. Tomorrow she'll be present.

But she knows, she knows, even as she thinks this, makes this promise to herself and to her sleeping daughter, you can make all the plans you want for the next day and it will still catch you on autopilot.

Celia rolls over and buries her head into Natha's breasts.

Tomorrow she'll take Celia to the park and take her camera in case Celia should make another sand pie. Celia will know it was there, that it was real. Real, like the walk she took with John Gulliver today. She rubs Celia's back. Thank God, she has this child. Poor John without the one born to him.

She could still give him a child.

She could bring him to ecstasy.

It's dangerous to think this way.

She could.

She feels a combination of excitement and fear.

Didn't he say that? When they were standing at her car, saying goodbye.

She remembers his mouth moving.

She remembers standing there for a long time.

What was he saying?

She is tired now. It's been a stressful day. A stressful night.

Tomorrow, she'll try to remember what exactly it was John said.

The shadows in the room, cast by the night light, tell her there *was* more to it. More than just goodbye. She's supposed to call him, to hear more of the story. That she remembers.

Tomorrow, she'll call him; if Devon is going to be away, she can ask John to drop by.

More attentive to Celia. The park. The bath.

Call John.

That's enough for now, she thinks, drifting. Everything can wait. For now, what matters are the shampooed little-girl hair and soft breaths at her breast.

She only wants to be here now, leave everything for the next day.

The smell of the shampoo. The flash of blond hair. She knows on some level that the smell of shampoo has something to do with Darlene, Buddy Francis's daughter. She knows they were young, that she was in the kitchen of his house washing something out of Darlene's hair. She knows her own hands were young, no bigger than Celia's.

She doesn't want to think past that. Not tonight. And not tomorrow. Some things you don't want to face the next day.

It could be the fast pounding of her own heart that wakes Celia.

"Mommy," she says sleepily.

"I'm here, sweet girl. Go back to sleep."

"Baby-loves-the-Mama," Celia sings.

"Mama-loves-the-baby," Natha sings back. Tears rest on the early morning side of the night. What was it John said? "Love matters?" It matters most, she thinks, when you realize you haven't let it matter enough.

THIRTEEN

"CAN YOU STICK AROUND today? Keep an eye on the roofer?" Devon asks while he throws some clothes into a duffle bag. He's angry this morning. She didn't go to their sacred marriage bed last night.

"I need to get some groceries, but other than that I'll stick around," she says, making the bed to avoid eye contact.

"That includes not hanging out with some hotshot auctioneer," he adds, scathingly.

"But it's okay for you to spend nights at your girlfriend's," she shoots back.

He falls silent, pulls the zipper shut with violence.

"C'mon, Devon. Let's not go away angry."

"You're the one who didn't come to bed last night, Natha."

"I needed time with Celia. I fell asleep. I did work last night."

There's anger in her own voice and it pisses her off. It's no way to start the day — the next day. She walks over to Devon and puts her arms around him but she feels nothing. He, on the other hand, takes her into his arms welcomingly and kisses her as though she's his possession, his hands sliding down her backside. She pulls away.

"I have to get Celia ready for school."

"We'll finish this when I get home," he says.

When he gets home. She won't let herself think that far ahead. Right now, she just wants him gone. She needs some time to herself, to think. There's the question of when she'll see Jules next and what part of John's story about Cup and Saucer she'll tell him.

By the time she arrives home, after taking Celia to school, there are two men tearing the old shingles off the roof, scattering them and the last twenty years onto the front lawn. Irene had to replace the roof after Ray Cole left. Natha was fifteen and had just started having sex with Jules. It's too crazy that it can be happening again.

Gord, a small man with a two-day growth of beard on his face, waves hello. She has seen him before, over for a beer in the garage with some of Devon's acquaintances. The larger man next to him seems familiar, but she cannot place him. She doesn't bother to chat with the men and heads inside to check her email. To her surprise, there is a reply from Dr. David Riddell; he tells her to look up the word *psychometry*, that aside from it meaning a measurement of mental abilities, it also means divination of facts concerning an object from contact with it. *Some people have this ability*, he writes. *Where are you?*

She thinks of another question, but the phone rings before she can type it out.

"It's Mum," Irene says. "Are you coming up today? I need some rye."

"The roof is being fixed today so I can't," Natha tells her.

"What's wrong with the roof?"

"It leaks. It's been twenty years since it was last replaced."

"Jesus Christ. That long?"

"I was fifteen. I remember. By the way, I've something to ask you."

"You need money."

"No. I can handle it. I wanted to ask you. Are you sure I was at Buddy Francis's house when I was young?"

Silence falls at the other end.

"Mother?"

"How the hell should I know?!" Irene shouts. "What bloody difference does it make?"

"I'm just asking a simple question," Natha says.

Her mother's anger causes her to be confused and worried. She ends the conversation without revealing this to Irene. The aluminum tray she made at fifteen is on the kitchen counter, leaning against the wall. She picks it up and tries to feel what she felt at fifteen. Nothing comes. She goes back to her desk and writes to Dr. Riddell. *Can we pick up on other's lives from objects? Can we take an emotion we have and purposely transfer it to an object to get rid of it? By the way*, she writes, *I'm from Stirling, Ontario, Canada*. She fires the email off before really thinking, hoping he'll answer. She can hear the men ripping the shingles off the roof as though it were right above her, not another floor up.

For the reconstruction of your life, she hears.

The woman's voice.

Her return is a bit of a surprise. So is the sudden appearance of Ruthie in the doorway. She hadn't even heard a knock.

"I hadn't heard from you in the last two days, love. I thought I'd come by and see if you're all right."

Ruthie sits down on the loveseat.

"God, I'm so sorry, Ruthie. I just, I just didn't even think. Fuck, I don't know what's wrong with me. It's like I'm forgetting about everyone I care about."

"What on earth are you talking about?"

Natha sits down on the couch and buries her head in her hands. First Celia. Now Ruthie.

"I don't know what it is. I'm just forgetting things — people. You."

"What's bothering you?"

"I don't know. It's like I'm remembering something but I don't know what."

"Oh, love," Ruthie says, walking over and sitting down beside her.

"What about your meals?" Natha asks. "How have you managed?"

"I've got other friends. Don't feel you have to help out so much."

"I saw John Gulliver. He told me a little. I'm not supposed to tell anyone but I know I can trust you."

"Something juicy?" Ruthie asks.

"No. Oh, I can't think right now. He said a lot of things. Do you want some coffee?"

"That, and can you sew a button on a shirt?" she asks, pulling one out of her bag. "I didn't know you were getting your roof done."

"I thought I told you I needed money. That's why I went to see Jules."

"Oh, that's right. God, aren't we a pair. Neither one of us can remember anything."

She follows Natha into the kitchen.

"The noise is driving me crazy," she tells Ruthie.

"I hope you don't plan to be here all day, listening to this."

Natha fills the coffee maker with water, scoops coffee into the filter.

"I don't think I can bear it, Ruthie. I might go to my mother's. Want to come?"

"To your mother's?"

"For a swim. We'll surprise her."

"You've never invited me there."

"That's because I think she's jealous of you."

"I'm not sure I want to meet her."

"C'mon."

"Let's have the coffee first. But I can't swim with this," Ruthie says, pointing to the sling on her shoulder.

"Christ, Ruthie. I am losing it. "

"I really want you to remember what John told you."

"I can tell you he said to me, 'Don't do anything to make me fall for you.'"

"He did not!"

"He did. Crazy, isn't it?"

"That he'd fall for you? That's not crazy at all. I told you. I have a feeling about this. Actually, I have a feeling about you."

"Me? Well, something is going on. It's like someone stepped on the gas pedal of my life. Things are racing. I don't know why."

Ruthie rests a hand on Natha's knee.

"He said something happened in Christina's house."

"Christina? Jack's lover?"

"Yes. I need to find out what. I think I'm going to tell the story to Jules as it was. I just don't think it would ring true otherwise. I know this sounds strange, but I think the roof is being replaced now for a reason."

Ruthie gives her a quizzical look.

"The roof?" she asks.

"Yes."

"What is it you're remembering?"

Natha shudders.

"I don't want to remember. Something from when I was young — Celia's age, I think. And I think my mother knows. I think the coffee's ready."

Ruthie follows her back into the kitchen. There's something in Ruthie's eyes that makes Natha think Ruthie already knows what she's talking about. But it can't be, she tells herself. How could she? Still, the look. It's fearful.

"John has this photographic memory," she tells Ruthie. "He recited a note that Jack gave to Christina. How the air went out of him every time she left a sale. She collected cups and saucers. Did I tell you? That's what they called each other."

"You did. How long did the affair go on?"

"I don't know." Natha pours two mugs of coffee and sets out milk and sugar. "Do you think we can transfer our emotions to objects?"

"What on earth are you talking about?"

"There are tests for telling if you can feel other people's

lives in an object. I've been emailing this scientist in the States. He studies it. God, can you imagine how many lives John Gulliver walks around with?"

"A scientist?"

"It's called 'psychometry.' Maybe I should see Jules today."

Ruthie follows Natha into the living room again.

"You're all over the place, love."

"Scattered. I know. I don't know why."

Natha notices a white thread on her jeans. She pulls it off and holds it up.

"I'm unravelling," she laughs.

"Do you like this John Gulliver?"

"He makes me feel. I can't dissociate so easily with him. And it worries me."

"Don't see him."

"I need the story."

"Make one up."

"I don't want to. I want to know now what happened. Besides, I like being with him."

"You seem a little derailed, Natha. I'm concerned."

"That's exactly how I feel. Now that I think about it, that's the word John used. We were standing by my car saying goodbye and he was talking and his words were going in and out. I must have shut down. He said something about not wanting to be derailed by this."

Natha rubs her forehead. The tightening sensation is back.

"Do you have a headache?"

Natha lets out a sigh.

"I move in and out of being present. One minute I'm

here and the next I'm strangely outside of myself."

Ruthie drinks her coffee and looks at Natha, into her eyes. "John touched me. Brushed my hair out of my face. I told him he makes me feel like I've never been touched before. I think I said that. I don't remember what he said, if he said anything at all. Could I actually have said that?"

Natha hears the sound of nails being pried out of place, the shingles sliding off the roof, landing on the front lawn.

"I can't bear to be here anymore. I just can't decide — my mother's or Jules's."

"Personally, love, I don't think either one is a good choice. Not the way you're feeling."

Natha stands with her cup in her hand.

"Can I see you tomorrow, Ruthie? I really need to get out of here."

Ruthie puts the shirt, still without its button, back in her bag. She follows Natha into the kitchen.

"Do you want to come to my place?" Ruthie offers.

"No. I have this need to get something done. I'll see you later. Shit, I didn't sew that button on for you."

"Another time, love. It's not urgent."

That's the word, Natha thinks, after Ruthie closes the door. She feels an urgency, like something is urgent, but she doesn't know what. Her pulse is racing. Didn't John say there's something about her that makes this all right? Yes, by the car, before she left. How long were they standing there? All she knows now is she can't stay in a house that's being ripped apart. She grabs her cigarettes and heads out the door.

OAK LAKE IS CALM and flat. They say it is spring-fed by arte-
sian streams that run deep below the surface of the hills. Even
during storms it is relatively calm. Natha glances at it and
wishes for the ocean, something with more life. Irene seems
content to stare at this puddle of a lake for the rest of her
life. It is enough life for her, the neighbourhood of cottagers
and homeowners, a two-minute drive into town, where the
liquor store is. The same town she's lived in for sixty years.

This morning, even the town seems to be in a state of
urgency to Natha. People look at her in her car as if they
know something, where she is headed, what it is she needs to
know. She sees a licence plate on another car, BRV HRT. *Because
your heart is brave.* The man behind the wheel waves as he
passes her.

IRENE OFFERS HER CHAMPAGNE and orange juice, a substitute
for the morning Caesars, the hard liquor kept waiting for the
hard part of the day — the stretch of the afternoon in the
harsh and truthful light. Natha didn't think to stop and get rye.
The champagne seems strangely fitting, that this is an occasion
of some kind. But it's not the real stuff. That's too expensive.
To her own surprise she accepts Irene's offer.

"Where's Clyde today?" Natha asks. He never seems to be
around anymore.

"Golfing," Irene answers, boredom in her voice. "The bugger
won't carry a cellphone so I couldn't call him to pick up some
rye. And, of course, you didn't think of it."

"I'm sorry. I've got other things on my mind today."

Natha hopes by the tone in her voice that she has implied

that there's a reason she's here. As Irene prattles on about this neighbour and that neighbour, Natha watches her, observes the silence between stories and the way her mother's mouth hangs open. She knows it is her mother — the same old Irene — but she feels like a complete stranger with a mouth that speaks of nothing, mumbled garbled words that echo in Natha's ears.

"Did you hear what I said?" Irene asks, sharply, loudly. "Your father never liked coming up to the lake."

Irene lights a cigarette and smokes it anxiously.

"Your father didn't like a lot of things," she adds, looking straight out at the lake as if she's talking to no one in particular. It makes Natha feel invisible, but she stays silent. Perhaps Irene is referring to sex, that Daddy didn't like sex. Maybe that's the way she sees it.

"Your father also liked some things a little too much, like his drink and his buddies. They always came first."

"Like Buddy Francis?"

Irene looks Natha in the eye with defeat. She swallows hard. Natha isn't sure, but are there tears in her mother's eyes, bloodshot as they are?

"I only let you go there once," she says. "Just once. Your father was very drunk that day, claimed he passed out there but woke up and thought he saw something. He convinced himself it was some kind of hallucination and he stayed friends with that bastard. But I knew."

"Knew what?" Natha asks, not wanting to know, but wanting to know. She takes a long chug of the champagne and orange juice. She's never known her heart to race so fast.

She tries to steel herself, stiffen her back, but sitting down doesn't help. She stands up, flexes her spine.

"I knew what happened that day," Irene says. "I don't want to talk about the details. It makes me sick. But I knew."

"How did you know, Mother?"

Irene lets out a long sigh.

"You never needed me, or anyone, after that. You changed."

"How old was I?"

"Celia's age. You favoured your father, I know. But that son of a bitch didn't do you any good. Not that day. Not ever."

There is anger in Irene's voice.

Now there *are* tears in her eyes and she wipes them with the back of her hand, reaches for her drink. Natha doesn't know what to do, to touch her or walk away. She wants to feel anger herself, but it is only the dread she feels, like the whole thing is about to happen again, or for the first time. Now her life feels like one long rape and it bothers her terribly that she can't think of what happened. Was she raped? She couldn't have been, not vaginally. Jules was the one who broke her hymen. Christ, it is coming to her now, that it must have been her mouth. And what was it she was washing out of little Darlene's hair? A stream of confusion and images runs through her mind. She sees Irene burying her head in her hands.

"Maybe I shouldn't have said anything," Irene says softly. "I've waited twenty years to let that out. To tell you that I understand why you are the way you are. Christ, I missed my little girl," she cries out.

"I don't think I was ever little," is all Natha can say. "I'm going to go now, Mother. I need to be alone for a while."

"I shouldn't have said anything, but you kept asking me."

Irene rises out of her chair and walks over to Natha. She puts a reluctant hand on Natha's arm. Natha wants to photograph this — her mother's hand on her arm. The touch.

"Tell me I did the right thing," Irene pleads. "Tell me I won't have to pay for it any longer."

Irene looks so tiny, too small to consume all the booze she puts down in a day. She's been drowning, Natha thinks, drowning by a lake without getting wet. But her sobriety today is what scares Natha. Too tipsy to drive into town for more rye. Too straight and serious to fall down in a drunken heap.

"Like you said, I've been asking," Natha tells her. She can't bring herself to hug her mother. Just the thought of touching anyone, of embracing another body, is too much.

"I'm going to go now," she repeats while Irene's hand falls from her arm.

"I understand," Irene says, the air going out of her. "I'm going to go and finish my drink."

Natha walks away from Irene, following the dirt path back to her car. This isn't what she had planned for today. More attention to Celia. Be present. Take care of Ruthie. Call John. She feels like she's been jerked into another reality. Even the potholes in the cottage road hurt her, jerking the car violently as she makes her way home. She has to keep it together for Celia's sake. So she tells herself. There's the bank to go to, to cash Jules's cheque, and the money from the sex with Stephen to deposit. And there's the grocery store. She needs some food. There are things to take care of. She'll not let this get in the way. Besides, it doesn't quite seem real. She can't remember it. It's like it happened to someone else.

Winding into town, she heads home to get the cheque and the money, the sound of the shingles coming off the roof only serve to keep her adrenaline going. In her bedroom she sees that Devon has thrown a pair of dirty jeans on the floor. She picks them up. She hasn't been able to flesh Devon out lately. It's like he doesn't exist in her world. Even the hug she gave him today was like wrapping her arms around an old ornament — an object. The jeans hang limp in her hand and Devon disappears from her mind when she puts them in the laundry basket. There's no cleaning Devon up — making him care, really care — and she knows that. Now on to the tasks at hand.

The bank.

The grocery store.

Maybe Jules's place.

The heat of the day has spiked. At the bank, the air conditioning is on the fritz. She stands in line waving the cheque like a fan in front of her face. Today, of all days, she wants to get this over with quickly. She's not used to having a cheque written out to her. The teller will surely know the name. Everyone in town knows Jules.

It is Nancy, a heavy-set woman in her mid-fifties with curled auburn hair.

"Jules Moore," she comments while she looks at the cheque. "Too bad about him."

Natha thinks, *What can I say?* There'll be another cheque and the tellers will surely gossip. She could say she's doing some work for him, but that will only lead to another question.

And another. And comments. *Poor Jules Moore.* She doesn't say anything. She watches Nancy stamp the cheque and the deposit slip; she turns to the computer and her long, red nails catch Natha's attention. They're long, like claws.

Claw your way out.

Wherever this voice is coming from, it's fitting and all-knowing, all-seeing. *How can we just make up the sound of someone else's voice?* Natha wonders. It must be a real person's voice — something she heard one time. Or something just given to her. Wherever it's coming from, she trusts it. She does have to claw her way out of the dread that has settled and infested this bright June day.

"We hardly see Jules anymore," Nancy says. "Say hello to him for me."

With that, Natha leaves with a grocery list running through her mind. What was it she needed?

Cereal.

Milk.

Deli meat.

When she gets back into her car, she lights a cigarette. A feeling of euphoria takes over. Now she knows. Now she knows she wasn't losing her mind remembering young Darlene and a sick feeling. Something bad had happened. Now she knows why she is the way she is, like Irene said. It flattens the shock of it even though it still feels like it happened to someone else.

Of course it happened to someone else.

She was a little girl.

She was different then.

Yes, she thinks. *Then. Not now.*

No sooner though does she feel this way than Celia's young face comes into her mind. She continues driving to Foodland, just around the corner, passing the school along the way. *She was Celia's age.*

Hang on. Not now. Not now.

She feels as though her heart will burst through her chest. It's pounding. Her pulse is racing. She's sweating. *Keep it together*, she tells herself when she grabs a basket and heads for the aisle with cereal, all the while feeling as though everyone in the store knows the kind of morning she has had. She perceives a "cheered on feeling" coming from nods of hello and sympathetic smiles. She grabs a box of Cheerios, not thinking twice about it even though it's not the kind she usually buys. For the occasion, she thinks. For luck.

Fuck.

"Deborah the deli woman," she distractedly blurts out when she sees her at the counter, then regrets it. What a label for someone so nice, so generous. She silently kicks herself for it.

"That's me," Deborah says, jokingly, holding up a ham.

If only Natha could laugh.

"I'm sorry," she says. "It's my way of keeping things straight. I'm losing my mind."

"Aren't we all, Natha. Say — now that you're here. How about coming over after school for a play date with your daughter? I'm off at three."

"I don't know. Today's not the greatest day," Natha tells her. "Can I have 300 grams of the Black Forest ham, please?"

Deborah looks disappointed as she slices the meat. Celia

will be too, Natha thinks, and today she's supposed to be more attentive to Celia. Why should Celia have to pay for what's happened to Natha today?

"Actually," Natha corrects herself. "Today would be fine. I'll see you then."

"Wait," Deborah says. "You're forgetting your ham."

She hands it to Natha and gives her a concerned look.

You never were a ham.

"No, I wasn't," Natha says under her breath.

"I'm sorry. I didn't hear you," Deborah tells her.

"Nothing. Just mumbling to myself."

"Are you all right?"

"I'm fine. Really. I'll see you later."

The distance from the deli to the dairy section is painstakingly long — the other side of the store. Natha can't remember it ever taking this long as a band above her eyebrows aches and she stops to rub her forehead. She feels like vomiting and breathes deeply to keep it from coming up.

Not now, not now.

By the time Natha gets the milk and then pays for her groceries, it feels like an hour has gone by. It's only been a matter of minutes. Her life seemed to be racing out of control before today. Now it seems to be crawling. All she wants now is to make it to the next day again. On the drive home, the town feels like a film set. She feels herself cast accidentally in some movie she doesn't want to be in. Thankfully, the roofers have taken a break for lunch. The house on Edward Street is quiet and still. She is torn between her desire to sleep and the need to keep moving. The in-between is excruciating. She plops down on the couch, stares at the books still sitting on the table. Virginia. Anaïs. Sylvia.

You have a story of your own.

She tries to put that idea out of her mind, and wonders if Jules might be home. She can tell him a story and make some money. Better than brooding, she tells herself. She realizes she hasn't eaten all day, but can't bring herself to make a sandwich or get a bowl of cereal. Instead, she pours herself a glass of white wine and takes it and her cigarettes outside to the picnic table, stepping over a jumble of shingles on the lawn.

The first glass of wine settles her pulse, the second puts distance between now and when she spoke to Irene, distancing herself from the disclosure further and further. It also brings into focus more of her conversation with John Gulliver, when they were walking down the road, when she was listening to the birds. Now she recalls that he said how hard it will be not to fall for her. Yes, he said that. That he thinks about her all the time. That that's how it was with Jack and Christina, in between the auction sales, Jack told John he could not get Christina out of his mind. John said to Natha, "I want something different with you. Not a tragic ending."

She's sure now that he said that, that he wants a different ending. She must have shut down, couldn't take it in until now, with the wine and the roof of the house she's always lived in torn apart, the debris beneath her feet. *You see more clearly in disruption*, she thinks. She sees *repair* as the key word of the day. The bald roof is proof to her that, if nothing else, she needs to repair her life and she can't do it without money. She finishes the last drops of wine before heading off to

Jules's house. The fallen woman sculpture at Ruthie's is on her mind, the aluminum tray, the shingleless roof have all become objects of significance and meaning. A Royal Doulton girl stands waiting on the other side of town — the one with the red pinafore.

FOURTEEN

"Y OU ASKED ME WHAT I know about love," Natha says from her seat in the living room. Jules pours cognac for her unexpected arrival.

"Back so soon," he said at the door.

"I'll tell you a story, Jules. But you must promise not to tell anyone."

"Who am I going to tell?" he asks, carrying the two glasses. "And I'll be dead soon, as you know. So don't skip the juicy parts."

"I already told you I met someone," she starts. It was on the way over in the car that she decided on making herself the central character — making someone else's story her own. It just came to her that it should come out in first person. "He's an auctioneer," she continues. "We met at one of his sales — before the sale started."

She remembers how Virginia Woolf closely wove her own life into her stories, how blatantly honest Plath was — even Anaïs Nin couldn't resist putting something of herself and others she knew into her work. Reading their diaries and journals has taught Natha this, and she can put it to use herself now. Besides: she has met someone and they did meet at one of his sales.

She throws the line between reality and fiction out the living room window and tells Jules that they began passing notes to one another at other sales, that he calls her "Cup" and she calls him "Saucer." Jules listens intently and gives her the odd *I'm-not-sure-I-believe-this* look. At least, that what she believes she's seeing.

"Are we talking about that John Gulliver fellow?" he asks.

"That, I won't tell you," she answers. "He's not the only auctioneer in this area."

"Is this person married?"

"Yes, he is. But then, so am I. That's beside the point. The point is he seemed to know early on that something was going to happen between us. He as much as said so. Told me to not do anything to make him fall for me. Then the next minute, he told me it was going to be hard not to fall for me. I thought it was all some kind of joke. But he was being honest. He's an honest man. Things just happened between us."

"Cup and Saucer. You don't expect me to believe those pet names."

"I collect teacups and saucers. It seemed appropriate."

"What was in the notes?"

"When we'd meet next. Phone calls were out of the question. Because of Devon and because of his wife. Whenever I left a sale while it was still on, he told me the air went right out of him. He's a poetic man. And before me, he was the salt of the earth."

"And because he was an honest man, you decided you liked him?"

"Because he's real."

"And all the other men you've been with aren't? C'mon, Natha, he's no different than them."

"But he is. And I'll tell you why later. Will you be writing another cheque for me today?"

"Just for that?"

"For the first instalment. There's a lot more to the story. I promise it's worth hearing."

"What about what else I want?"

"In time," she says.

"Don't have much of that. Besides, why not now?"

"But you seemed as much interested in knowing what I know about love."

"I am. I don't believe you know anything."

"That's where you're wrong. And I'll prove it. Just not today. Another cheque and I'll be back."

She can't think of what else to say, or she'd say it now. She needs time to figure out the rest of the story she'll tell him. Besides, what *does* she know about love?

Jules rests a hand on his crotch.

"I need you to try," he says. "In the bedroom, not out here with the curtains wide open. C'mon," he says, half standing, half hunched over.

"No," she says. "It has to be here. I'm not going to your bed again."

"Then I'll close the curtains."

"I don't want to do this today," she tells him.

"But you want a cheque. I'll make it for five thousand today and the rest when you tell me the rest of the story."

Now she doesn't know what to do. If she hadn't had the morning she's had, it wouldn't be so hard. She can feel the clamps around her forehead and her stomach is unsettled.

Not now, not now.

She catches a glimpse of the Royal Doulton figurine — the girl with the swaying red pinafore. What difference does it make anymore, anyway? She remembers she used to have a pet name for her but can't remember what it was. Jules closes the curtains, then sits back down in his seat and unzips his pants, pulls out his limp penis and begins stroking it.

Nothing happens.

"I can't do it on my own," he says. "Five thousand."

"Do you think it's just magically going to happen?" she asks. "You're setting yourself up, Jules."

"If anyone can do that, Natha, you can."

He pulls his pants down.

Pathetic, she thinks.

She'll have to get Celia from school soon.

Celia.

Think of Celia.

She can't believe Irene didn't say anything until now.

And goddamn Daddy.

No, I'm not all right, you bastard.

She gets up from her seat and sits down beside Jules, staring into his naked lap. She can do this, she tells herself, and when she rests a hand on his penis she is relieved to see it is her adult hand, not her child hand.

"Use your mouth," Jules asks softly.

"Not yet," she tells him.

She strokes his penis and all she feels is limp, weak flesh.

"This just shows you that I'm willing," she says. Then she stands up abruptly.

"You know better than this, Jules. I don't do anything until I get the money first."

"Fine," he says. "Bring me my chequebook out of the desk. And you still have to tell me how you feel about me dying."

She ignores that last part and walks over and opens the top drawer and finds the chequebook right on top, grabs a pen from the holder, and returns to him, watches him write it out.

Pathetic, she thinks again; half naked and writing a cheque as if some miracle is going to happen.

She looks at the clock on top of the television. She has less than an hour to get this over with.

Can she do it?

Irene's tears seemed genuine.

How could Daddy be so drunk?

It all runs through her mind, and Buddy Francis's living room with its gold shag carpet and brown plaid rocker. Another naked lap. Another cock, fat and throbbing.

Christ.

Jules finishes writing the cheque and hands it to her. He's got it all correct — the amount, the date, his signature.

She swallows hard and then realizes she won't be swallowing

anything. There's no way he'll come. This realization makes her lower her head to his lap.

"My lover loves when I do this to him," she whispers.

Jules puts his hands on her head, pushing her down.

"Show me," he says. "Show me now."

She puts her mouth around him and he lets out a moan. Nothing happens for the longest time but she keeps on wanting this to make her remember what happened when she was young. She expects an image to come at any moment but when she closes her eyes she only sees herself at this age sucking the cock of an old and fragile Jules, while she feels John Gulliver's touch across her face. She thinks of Daddy when he was drunk. Can a man like John Gulliver love her? Can she change her life?

"Just keep trying," Jules says, holding her head close to him.

But it's no use, she knows, and she forces his hands away and sits back up.

"I tried," she tells him. "I've more than made my money today."

She stands up and puts the cheque in the pocket of her jeans.

"If you try again, I'll write you another cheque," Jules promises.

"I'll be back again. Soon," she says. "I'll tell you the rest of the story then."

She flings the curtains wide open and walks out of the house.

IN HER CAR, SHE lights a cigarette, takes a few long drags. It is disappointing that she made herself do it and nothing happened. No big flashback. Not even a queasy feeling. It's like it never happened, but it happened — Irene was proof today. Daddy's long disappearance is proof.

Shit.

It's like being part of a story you can't remembering starring in, but everyone has their own version. Daddy's version was silent, Irene's booze-laden. Whatever happened to Darlene? she wonders. She remembers she moved to her mother's shortly after what happened. Just disappeared. Only Buddy Francis is still around and Natha can picture him waving to her at that auction sale not long ago.

Before she pulls the car out of the driveway, Jules is standing in the living-room window with a smile on his face, waving to her as if she had just cleaned his house and serviced him.

Die, she wants to shout at him. *Just die.*

She stops at the bank again and deposits the cheque. Then she drives home, coming to a full stop on Mill Street, and finds herself staring at the stop sign in front of her.

Stop. Stop everything.

It's only when the car behind honks its horn that she proceeds, feeling like she's leaving something behind. She parks the car at home and walks to the school to get Celia. When she arrives, Celia hands her a picture she drew — a house without a roof, a Mommy and daughter in the upstairs bedroom, the Daddy passed out on the couch.

IN THE LATE AFTERNOON, she arrives at Deborah's as much for herself as for Celia, the walls of her own house having closed in on her in the half-hour spent at home after school.

Celia had pulled out a box of her favourite things, but it was full of triggers for Natha, the woman's voice in her head providing a running commentary on every little thing.

"Mommy," Celia said, "Remember this feather?"

Flight. Flying. "The robin's feather," she said. "Look at all this stuff from my treasure box."

There wasn't any chance that the objects Celia pulled out were random and meaningless.

The small silver crown.

A hatless acorn.

They'll all be taking their hats off for you.

"Are you trying to help me?" Natha asked Celia, certain that her daughter knew something.

"Yes," Celia said.

Now she's on the living room floor of Deborah's house, playing Twister with Deborah's daughter, Amber.

Twisted as your marriage.

"A glass of wine?" Deborah asks.

"Sure, why not?"

Still feeling the effects of the earlier wine and the cognac at Jules's, Natha figures she'll relax with yet another drink. Maybe the voice will go away and she'll be able to push herself out beyond everything.

She can see by the meagre furniture and the cheap drapes on the windows that Deborah doesn't have much money. Still, it feels like home, like a safe place. Amber and Celia are playing well and Natha welcomes the break.

Breathe, she tells herself.

Deborah's younger sister, the one who sold Natha the

teacups and saucers the day of the yard sale, comes home and goes right to her room.

"Never mind her," Deborah says, setting down the wine on the dining room table. "She's not anti-social, just shy."

There is still something very familiar about the sister to Natha. She shrugs it off, takes a long sip of the wine.

"I can really use this," she tells Deborah. "Thanks."

"Rough day?"

"I'm trying to push myself out beyond it."

"And how hard is that?"

"I've been doing it for years. It's all in the breathing, picturing a small you inside and imagining it getting bigger with every exhale until it gets bigger than you and enters the vast blue light that surrounds you."

"You seem really serious about it."

"I am. I can usually push myself out beyond everything and it all just bounces off the blue light."

"Sounds New Age to me."

"I was doing it before New Age became popular."

"Something you made up?"

"As a matter of fact, yes."

"I knew you were going to be an interesting person."

"Not really."

"There's something mysterious about you," Deborah teases, hinting she wants to know more.

"Please," Natha says, hoping to end it there.

She can feel the alcohol spreading through her blood and into her limbs and her chest. Now she knows why she didn't want to come here before; there's an expectation that she will share the narrative arc of her life, everything before this moment to be offered up for the taking. It all weighs so much and she can't find any words to start, let alone dole it out in chapters.

"Why Stirling?" Natha asks Deborah, to switch subjects.

"My mother lived in this area before. She wanted to come back. Although, now she's blind and can't see it the way it is today. It was almost twenty years ago that she left. So there's that. And the fact my husband split last year. All in all, there was nothing keeping us in Cobourg. My father died years ago. So the four of us came here."

"Your mother lives here then?"

"She spends most of her time in her room, reading Braille and listening to opera. So, tell me about your husband, Natha. How long have you been together?"

"It's not such an interesting subject at the moment," Natha says, dismissively, without wanting to sound impolite. She likes this Deborah and that she is struggling to make a home. Another fallen woman picking herself up, she thinks.

Deborah takes Natha's cue. "So, you just picture it? That's all there is to it? You imagine yourself small, and then you imagine yourself growing and growing?"

"You have to want it. You have to be willing to let go of everything, and I mean everything."

"And you've really been able to do it?"

"For years. I can teach you. I can teach anyone."

"Think of all the good that would do. If someone's sick, or if someone's hurting emotionally."

"Now you've got the idea. Believe me, I've pushed out

beyond all sorts of things you wouldn't want to experience."

"They should study you," Deborah says, enthusiastically.

Natha laughs.

"No — I'm serious. The thought of even doing such a thing would never enter most people's minds. And it's so simple. Does it really work?"

Natha wants to say yes, that even the knowledge of being abused as a child bounces off the vast blue light surrounding her, if she could only summon it. Even though it still feels like it happened to someone else, it sits there on her shoulders, ugly and sickening, especially watching Celia and Amber in the other room, living only in the moment, trustingly.

Celia runs over, panting happily.

"Mommy, come play Twister," she pleads.

"I don't think so, sweet girl."

"Come on," Deborah says, standing up. "Come on, it'll be fun."

Natha downs the last of her wine and walks reluctantly over to the plastic sheet on the living room floor.

"Okay," Deborah says. "We're going to be serious. We are going to play by the instructions." She spins the dial. "Natha, put your right foot on red."

As she twists with a foot on red and the other on blue and a hand on green, almost toppling over, trying hard to maintain some kind of balance, she realizes it's the cliché of her life she doesn't want Deborah to know. A sexually abused girl who becomes a hooker. Christ, she thinks, she can't stand clichés in literature, but in life she's a cardboard cutout of a prostitute. She's never wanted to be a cliché of any kind of woman; she always thought she was a woman of independence, that her lifestyle was of her own choosing, not the result of some childhood nightmare. What to do with it, she wonders, while Celia joins her on the plastic sheet, sticking a foot under Natha's ribs. Another stretch of Celia's right hand puts Natha off balance completely and she falls on top of her daughter.

Celia laughs and then the tears start.

She has hurt her.

She thought she felt her chin going into Celia's head.

Shit.

She pulls Celia into her chest and strokes her hair, "Sorry, sorry, sorry."

That's when it comes.

No one held her after.

She can feel the coldness that embraced her.

More than the physical pain, Natha senses in Celia that she has been offended, as if the fall were intentional.

"It was an accident, my girl."

There are no accidents.

Fuck off, she says to the voice.

"JOHN, I NEED TO see you," she says into the phone.

Back at home, Celia is watching television after much cuddling and reassurance. Natha could only think, what happens to a child when there is intentional pain and cruelty?

"Tomorrow is my only day this week without a sale and I've got two listings to do."

"I really want to see you," she tries again.

There is a break of silence. All she can hear is Celia giggling over something on the television. "I can come by your house at nine-thirty. Just tell me where you live."

Crooked house. Edward Street.

The rest of the night she stays close to Celia, lying on the floor watching television, giving her a bath, sleeping next to her in the room where she herself returned after the day at Buddy Francis's house. It's a good thing she can't remember it exactly, staring at the slight slope in the ceiling. It's a good thing, this pushing out.

FIFTEEN

DAMAGED GOODS. NATHA AWAKENS to this thought of herself, relieved that Devon isn't beside her to comment on her mood. Depressed. Sad. Gloomy. Sometime in the middle of the night she left Celia's side and made her way across the hall to her own bed. The night is a blur; she was restless and struggled for sleep.

She wants to tell John Gulliver that she's lived too much to ever love someone. She wants to tell him about Buddy Francis and Jules Moore so that he knows there's a reason for such a statement.

She rolls over and doesn't want the day to start. Devon will be home this afternoon and she knows he's coming home to someone else. Something happened overnight, her insides scraped raw from yesterday, and her hangover doesn't help. But it's more than that. She's awakened to the startling idea that the things that have happened all happened to bring her to this point — the centre of her life where she can decide to make changes.

The birds chirping outside the nearest window tell her this is so. They are loud and gleeful and it rouses her out of bed with a sense of anticipation. She won't let Devon's coming home cloud this euphoric feeling. There'll be hats off to her if she just lets what needs to happen happen. Celia pulling the hatless acorn out of her treasure box was no coincidence. The Twister game and her twisted marriage. *There are no accidents.* That's what she heard. It's like the world is lining up to tell her something and there seem to be clues everywhere. Has she lived blindly all this time?

When Celia asks to take the long way to school, to go along Mill Street past the shops, Natha doesn't argue and has hardly a concern that they'll be a little late. She senses Celia is on her side. It is only when they turn the corner onto Mill and pass the feed mill that Natha loses any sensation of her body. Old Ted Thompson is inside the mill and when he waves she is certain there's a reason Celia wanted to go this way. Natha hasn't seen old Ted in years. He was Daddy's boss and must be eighty by now, she thinks. But it's the look on his face when he waves that gets her, like he's waving her on to something important.

They'll all wave and make room for you.

Make room for what, she wonders, holding Celia's hand, proudly walking as if the townsfolk are seeing her for the very first time. No more hiding behind the long hair and the clothes that don't fit well as she did when she was young. She talked to no one, not even when she was with Daddy.

Even though the stores aren't open yet, there are people in the street, nodding, *good morning, nice day*, friendlier than ever. She doesn't think that they might live in the apartments above the stores, or work at the odd office. She thinks they are there for her, to greet her on this day when everything can change. When a young man crosses from the opposite side of the street and walks past her, she is filled with the sense he just wanted to be near her. She tightens her grip on Celia's hand, not knowing if someone will come up to her, if she's supposed to meet up with someone who will tell her what to do next. Just then, a Wonder Bread delivery truck makes its way down the street towards the corner Mac's store and she takes it as a sign.

You'll no longer have to wonder where the bread will come from.

She can only take it that means Jules writing a big cheque. How to get him to write more? The truck only serves to heighten her euphoria: synchronicity is playing its great hand just for her.

But then, nothing.

They pass the rest of the stores and turn the corner and cross Church Street to Celia's school. When nothing meaningful happens the rest of the way, a feeling of great emptiness swells inside of her. Is she just imagining things? Her faith that the day will tell her what to do hangs like a white thread in the breezy morning air. There has to be meaning, she thinks, kissing Celia goodbye in the hall with all the other mothers and children she sees every day. Trust the voice, she tells herself as she leaves and begins her walk home. Trust the world.

"I PARKED DOWN THE street," John says. He leans against the counter. Here he is in the stark white kitchen wearing jeans and a white T-shirt. "You have to understand, I know too many people."

There's something very pure about the moment. About what he has just said. It tells her all she needs to know, that this is about more than just the story of Jack Callaberry and Christina Reid.

Natha stands across from him, leaning against the opposite counter, taking him in. He's not selling anything today and his words aren't up for bids. Christ, she thinks, his ways are as old as the antiques he sells — polite, honest, straight-forward. She wonders if he can see she has a desire to be the same way, at least the desire, even if she can't pull it off.

They move to the living room. She sits on the couch, expecting him to sit on the loveseat opposite her, but he sits beside her.

"Your house has that lived-in look," he tells her, smiling.

"You mean slightly messy?"

"Believe me, *this* is not messy. It's just right. Lived-in. You'd be surprised how many houses look like no one lives in them at all. The pillows are straightened, everything's cleared off the tables. I'm glad to see this. It makes me nervous when things are too neat."

"You strike me as extremely organized, John."

"Not in my home. Why did you need to see me?"

She isn't ready for that. She's still gathering information — his gestures say he's ready to hear anything, tapping her on the knee as he talks. But his hands seem a little shaky and he seems a little nervous, out of his element.

"Would your wife be upset that you're here?" she asks him.

"Are you kidding? Like I said, I know too many people and word can get back in ways you'd never think of."

"Well, like you said, you parked down the street. You're safe here."

"It's a nice house. Lived here long?"

"Practically all my life."

"And you got a new roof."

"Just yesterday. Except for the back. They'll be returning sometime today."

"Don't tell me it's Gord MacDonald doing it."

"Yes."

"Shit. He knows me. I did his father's auction."

"He probably won't come now. Relax."

"Why did you need to see me?"

She drops her head. She's not sure he's ready to hear the truth about her, if she can tell him the truth. When she lifts her head, some hair falls into her face. She sits there waiting to see if he'll do anything about it. A silence falls, except for the kitchen clock. It seems extraordinarily loud. She looks down at her hands. Inside she feels like a child waiting for approval; she half expects to see the hands of a child. But they're her adult hands — the hands that have touched many men in places she doesn't want to recall.

Then it comes. John's hand to brush away her hair. She stops it in mid-air and holds it. She wants to be touched and not be touched, and not be touched by him unless it's real.

"I've been in touch with this scientist in California about how some objects hold feelings, like they've taken on the lives of their previous owners. I wanted to tell you because I can feel the lives of people who've owned things from the past. It's called psychometry. His name is Dr. David Riddell. You can look him up."

John takes his hand away.

"You fascinate me," he says.

She smiles.

"I figure you can feel them too."

"I told you before, I'd be done if I did. The amount of shit I deal with."

"He studies people like me."

"What else can you do?"

"I can push myself out beyond everything."

"What are you talking about?"

"I can make it so I'm not affected by anything."

"Like I said, you fascinate me."

"I need to know what happened in Christina's house," she says. "You said something happened there."

His shoulders drop and his face becomes serious and strained. He starts playing with the cork coasters on the table.

"You really need to know?"

"You can't drop something like that and not tell me, John."

"You can't hold my hand like that and tell me there's nothing going on here."

"Do you want something to go on?"

He rises out of his seat and walks over to the bookcases.

"Someone does a lot of reading here."

"I do. Please come back and let's talk."

He stays near the bookcase.

"You want to know what happened? Why the love between them was so unbelievable?"

"Yes, I do."

"I've hardly told you how long their affair went on. Now you want the climax."

It doesn't escape her that Virginia and Sylvia and Anaïs are still sitting on the table beside her. It's like they're waiting for the story too, as if they could easily fill in the front end with a grand romance just to get to the unexpected twist in the story, if there is a twist.

"You said something went on in her house. What was it?"

John lets out a deep sigh. He looks her straight in the eye.

"You have to understand that I'm sharing someone else's intimate details here."

"I won't say anything to anyone."

"You can't. I'm trusting you."

"What happened?"

"Their affair was an emotional one, a long one. But he went to her house when her husband was at work one day and her daughter was in school. That's when it happened."

John shifts in his seat.

"They made love there," he says, searching out Natha's eyes. "Real love, not just sex. Jack said he never in his life felt such a joining with someone. It was unreal to him in many ways and he knew Christina felt the same."

Natha sits waiting for more, but John stays silent, looking like he's just told some deep, dark secret.

"That's it?" Natha asks. "They made love for the first time."

"The only time," John replies.

"Only one time."

"Yes. They sat afterwards at her kitchen table drinking tea and Jack told her all the things he wanted for them. He would leave his wife. They could move away, start over. But Christina's face fell and she became agitated."

"Didn't she love him?"

"Yes. More than anything, more than she knew possible. But she wanted it to just be about love. The lovemaking had changed everything. Now it was about what happens next. She couldn't break up her family for Jack, which is what he wanted. She wanted it to be pure, to just be. She didn't want to be acquired, like some kind of object."

"Love for love's sake. No promises, no mistakes, like you told me she said in that one note to him."

"Yes. Just before he left her house, she gave him the notes she had kept. She told him she wouldn't be coming to any more sales. She asked him to just love her anyway."

"I don't understand," Natha says. "At least I don't think I do."

"She wanted their love to be still, to just be. Don't you get that at all?"

"I don't know a lot about love," she says.

"Jack went through hell. He didn't see her at his sales and then he heard she was expecting another child. Christina and her husband moved away, and Jack couldn't live with that. Or without a child that might be his."

"That's what made him do it."

"He couldn't envision his life without Christina in it. Even having his own daughter wasn't enough to keep him from doing it. He was never right again."

"Why did you feel the need to tell me all of this?

"I thought maybe you'd feel the same way as Christina, about love being still. Do you think it's possible? I mean, you must know a lot about love."

"Me? I know very little."

She hesitates to go on, but the air is thick with all of this love talk and she can't resist.

"That time you brushed the hair out of my face, I told you that you make me feel like I've never been touched before. I meant that," she says.

She places a hand on his arm.

"I should go," he says abruptly, then walks out of the room.

She follows him into the kitchen.

"Wait, there's something else."

He turns around to face her.

"There can't be something else, Natha."

"Why not?"

"Because I could never share you."

"What do you mean?"

"Just that. I could never share you."

"You know."

"I know a lot about a lot of people."

The floor beneath her feet feels loose and wavy. She stands there, listening to him while the ceramic sun on the wall melts.

"I really need to go now," he says.

Her eyes settle on a rounded rock in the shape of an egg that sits on the table in the corner.

The birth rock for your rebirth.

All this time he knew.

All this time she was the one who thought she wasn't being honest. A flash of anger, and then she feels his arm again and he's still there and that's the thing, he was there even though he knew.

And now he is saying something — something she can't grasp, she can only see his mouth moving and the floor stays loose and wavy until he says it again.

"I really do have to go now."

Her hand falls from his arm as he pulls himself away and walks out the door. She goes to the window and watches him walk down the street. He makes his way quickly to his truck, looking around at the other houses as he walks.

When she walks back into the living room and sits down on the couch to just go over what has been said, she sees Virginia Woolf's diary, Volume Two, on the coffee table. Immediately she jumps up and searches on her computer for Virginia Woolf's voice and finds a recording from the BBC and hears her, dated and Edwardian and intellectual, speaking of writing, of telling the truth, of creating beauty. But Natha's concentration is off; it's too much to listen to the whole recording. She switches to her email. There she sees the answer to her question to Dr. David Riddell; he answers her that yes, we can transfer our emotions to objects. These can be called talismans. He thanks her for her interesting question, tells her he is studying this subject more and more these days, the energy of objects. Just as she signs out, the tapping on the roof begins, like some kind of signal to stop, stop everything. For the longest time, she lies on the couch listening to it, staring off into space, occasionally focusing on the old medicine cabinet and its nest of rocks.

She can't believe that all this time John knew about her.

Anger again.

I can really use someone like you in my life.

He said there can't be something between them.

She hears the footsteps of the roofers.

Never mind baby steps. Leap.

Leap where?

What else did John say in the kitchen while she stood there with her hand on his arm? For some reason, she can't bring it back. She only feels the band tightening around her forehead and her eyes blinking rapidly. Why can't she remember? She wants to remember. She wants to remember more than anything.

He did say other things while her hand was on his arm.

She is too tired now to go out, too anxious to stay in, the adrenaline pumping, her pulse racing. She could be mad as hell about John but she isn't. Instead, an overwhelming feeling that he said something about loving her. It's not so much that she can remember the words, only what she felt as he talked. She remembers him looking at her as if everything had changed, now that they'd said it, whatever it was.

Didn't he say his wife could make things difficult for her and for Celia, that she already suspects?

Natha remembers her at Piper's sale, weeks ago, waving him over while he stood beside Natha under the large maple in Piper's backyard. Piper's ticking watch that day was telling the correct time.

The tapping starts again and she realizes she has to escape.

Maybe the roofers saw him here. Maybe they know too.

The sunlight filters in through the living room window, creating beams of dust. She feels Christina's body being filled with Jack's love. If only John would come back now and fill her own body with honest love, really make love to her. Then she'd be rid of Jules and Buddy Francis, even Devon.

Shit, she thinks, he'll be here soon.

She'll go to Ruthie's.

Ruthie will understand these feelings she's experiencing — she wants to hide and sleep and she's experiencing the desire to leap into the mysterious, the unknown future where John Gulliver stands in kitchens to do listings on objects he refuses to feel and a scientist works diligently to figure out how some people can feel the life of them without even trying.

Just before leaving, she sends another email and tells David Riddell that not only can she feel the lives of the people who've owned objects, she can push herself out beyond everything and not feel anything.

THE DAY LOOKS DIFFERENT when she steps outside, the sun smiling on her achievements. She didn't push out. She let John know how she feels. Her skin tingles in the heat with the knowledge that life is opening up. She may have been one way all her life, shut off from much that has gone on, but on this day in June, even though she can't remember the date, she is finally letting herself feel fully. The only problem is that everyone seems to know. She can tell by the way people are looking at her. The man in his garden watering flowers can't help but ask her how she is on this fine day. He's never spoken to her before. A woman near the liquor store tells her the day is perfect for getting outside. *Outside of herself* is what Natha hears, from the voice inside that says, *They know and they're watching you.*

She wonders if Ruthie will notice too, if it's that evident that she sees the world differently now. The town falls in sync, like the perfect place for such an event to unfold. For her to unfold. Virginia Woolf would be especially happy that something this big is happening in such a small town. Natha, with her gifts, a woman no one would expect to feel this much love. She almost feels like she's walking on air, forgetting for a while that John said nothing could happen. Instead, she focuses on the fact he said he could never share her. That makes her feel important to him, that he needs her all to himself. Devon never could say it. He doesn't feel that way, she knows that. If only he would make it easy to let her go. Can the world make that happen too?

"THIS TIME I DIDN'T push out," she tells Ruthie.

Ruthie's eyes blink rapidly and Natha can see she's having a hard time understanding this.

"What did he say?" Ruthie asks.

"He said a lot," Natha answers, although all she can remember is that he couldn't share her. So she tells Ruthie, "He said he could never share me."

"You mean he knows about you."

"Yes."

"He said that?"

This frustrates Natha, this grilling. She lets out a sigh.

"He said a lot of things. I don't remember it all. But he knows and he still wants me, damaged goods that I am."

"You're not damaged goods, love."

"You don't know everything. I've been having memories of something that happened in my childhood. I was abused by a friend of my father's."

"Oh, love."

Ruthie puts a hand on Natha's knee.

"Irene remembers it too. She told me."

Natha stands and walks over to the fallen woman sculpture.

"I think I tried putting it here," she says, stroking it. "Do you believe we can do that? Transfer our feelings, like pain, to objects?"

"What are you talking about?"

"Dr. David Riddell — that scientist I told you about. He believes it."

"That one from California?"

"Yes. I need a cigarette."

Ruthie follows her out to the balcony and watches Natha as she takes long drags.

"Something big is happening," she says, staring at Ruthie, whose eyes continue to blink rapidly, as if she's hearing a story she doesn't quite believe. Natha senses this and feels uneasy. "I know it's hard to believe. All of this."

"All of what, love?"

"That this is happening," she says, impatiently. "With John Gulliver. With me. Maybe that's why everything in my life happened, to bring me to this point where I can know love, really know it."

She puts her cigarette out and lights another one. Ruthie's reaction is giving her a sinking feeling. Perhaps none of this is real. But it has to be, she thinks. John did come over. She feels the physical evidence. He came over. He sat on the couch beside her. She touched his hand and his arm. She could feel him. It's just overwhelming, she thinks, to realize the power of yourself, of your gifts, of your love. No wonder Ruthie doesn't understand.

"What are you going to do, love?" Ruthie finally asks, breaking the silence.

"I don't know," Natha says quietly, thinking of the voice, and wondering where it's gone. Sitting with Ruthie, it would be easy not to believe any of this, she thinks. Irene's words hover over her next thought, along with yesterday's stint with Jules, her mouth on him.

"I have to go, Ruthie. Devon will be home by now."

Ruthie follows her back into the apartment.

"I want to help you."

"Then don't act like you don't believe any of this," Natha snaps. She wastes no time leaving, walking home, looking for signs to tell her something. If what happened with Buddy Francis can be real, so can the rest of it. As for Jules, she can't stomach another try with his limp penis. She only wants John's mouth, John's body. Who was the father of Christina's baby?

The second floor of King's Mill comes to mind — the time she was inside, years ago, knowing of his death then and knowing of it now. How could it be that he made love to her for that reason? Did he feel wanted, or used?

Christina was honest in what she wanted.

She must be the same way, she thinks, passing Nancy Street where Deborah lives. Her younger sister, Stacey, comes to mind. Her face and her blond hair. Natha's steps quicken. She feels on the brink of some discovery, but can't quite catch it. She can't quite catch John's words either. The rest of the way home, she feels like she is reaching into a fog to recall what he said. The only thing that's clear as day is the sight of Devon's truck in the driveway, the roofers gone. She tries for a blank nothing look when she steps inside the kitchen and sees him standing over a sink full of fish.

"Who says I can't bring home the dinner?" he says, laughing.

Everyone will fish for answers.

He rinses his hands and dries them on a towel, standing proud of his catch, and all she can see is the eyes of the dead pickerel staring blankly.

"You survived without me, I see."

"I'm a survivor, yes, but you already know that about me," she says, sitting down at the kitchen table. He stands opposite her, staring. She avoids eye contact and picks up the birth rock, rolls it between her hands, as if it might take away all the anxiety she feels. Devon doesn't reach for her. She takes that as a sign. Maybe he knows. Maybe he is part of it. It seems an unlikely stretch, but then so does everything. How will she go from being a married hooker to the honest lover of an honest man? She doesn't know the next step, the next thing she's supposed to do.

Breathe, she tells herself.

Breathe, and wait.

"I brought you back something," he says, reaching into the pocket of his jeans. He pulls out the tiniest piece of driftwood.

Driftwood for the drifting she's done all these years.

It makes sense to her, this present. Like he's finally in step with her.

She wants to ask him if he went away to let all this happen. She wants to ask him if he'll let her go, but she stays silent, choosing to let it come from his mouth. A mouth she never wants to touch again. Can she believe him, even if he says he'll let her go? All these years of believing they were meant to live as they have. All the sex with others. It was meant to preserve them.

He never did say the sharing bothered him.

Not once.

Only that he had to be Number One.

One out of how many?

The clock ticks loudly from its place on the wall.

"Before I left, you didn't seem to want me to touch you. That kiss we had seemed cold, Natha. That's why I haven't hugged you yet."

This yanks her back.

Shit. He's not supposed to say this.

Maybe he doesn't know and she'll have to tell him. Tell him what, when she doesn't know herself? She puts the birth rock down and excuses herself to the bathroom. Before she reaches the top step in the hallway upstairs, the phone rings. She races to bedroom to get it before Devon.

It is Deborah, sounding breathless.

"You were supposed to call me, Natha."

"I was?"

"Yes, to let me know how Celia's doing. That and you're supposed to come for a visit, just the two of us."

All Natha hears are the words *supposed to call, supposed to come*, as though they're instructions. All morning she's been feeling like she's supposed to do things in order to be with John again, an odd feeling that's taken hold of her.

"I'm sorry."

Natha can't remember saying she would. She can't remember anything about what was said before she left Deborah's yesterday. She just remembers telling Celia *I'm sorry, I'm sorry*, holding her on the Twister sheet, trying to ease her pain.

"She's all better," she says.

"You sound confused, Natha. Come by and later we can go and get the kids from school. Besides, I can give you something for stress."

Anything to keep from being with Devon, Natha thinks. Is this where she's supposed to go next?

"Sure," she tells her. "I'll come now."

Hanging up, she sees Devon's duffle bag in the corner of the room by the closet.

Bags.

You'll be packing your bags, the two of you, and you and John will go far away.

Didn't he say this town's too small for something between them?

She's sure he said that, in the kitchen, before leaving.

She opens the bag and sees Devon's clothes ruffled and messily packed.

Ruffled.

She'll ruffle a few feathers by leaving.

Plummeting deeper into the certainty that everything she needs to know is being given to her, that life's clues are everywhere if we only take the time to see them, she leaves the house with the excuse that Deborah, her new friend, needs her. "What new friend?" Devon asks, but she is gone in a flash without an answer for him.

All it takes is to remove yourself. She makes tracks until she gets halfway down Edward Street, then slows, deciding to stop at Foodland to get brownies for the girls. Something tells her to take the long way, down Mill Street and around the corner. Outside, she can breathe in the humid air with relief that right now she doesn't need to perform as wife, as mother, as ... she just needs to walk. She lights a cigarette and the smell of the smoke is particularly strong — separate and distinctive, like the fresh–cut lawn she passes and the fresh dog shit near the sidewalk.

For all the shit she's been through.

It's her own voice she's hearing now.

What are the chances, she thinks, of meeting a man like John Gulliver who knows of a life like hers and still wants her?

"People like us find each other."

That's what he said. She's sure of it.

It's coming back to her while she contemplates calling him tonight and telling him she knows everything that's going on and that she can feel it moving through this town. She walks to the end of Edward Street and heads up Mill and feels a gust of braided nostalgia — strands of abandonment past the feed mill, smelling the oats of Daddy's presence, abandonment and elation that she is being thought of now by another, a decent man.

"I think of you often," John said.

A few farmers are gathered in the front of the feed mill, smoking; they part, making room for her. She sees a transport truck farther up the street, waiting at the light. The flashing signal on the truck catches her eye.

She hears the farmers laughing behind her. They all swore, years ago, they didn't have a clue where Daddy was, all they knew was that he went to Thunder Bay to drive a truck.

The word *dead* comes to mind, as the light changes and the truck chugs its way through the intersection. She has thought of it before. An accident?

The truck drives out of sight.

Just walk, she tells herself. Just keep walking.

The restaurant.

Stedman's, not called Stedman's anymore, but she can't remember its name.

The corner.

It's all just around the corner.

At the corner she turns right — right for the right way — passes the small bulk-food store with a slanted tin roof, pigeon shit on the sidewalk below it. She could keep to the right, but instead she crosses the street to the left to be on the side of Foodland and the gas station before it.

Because you've run out of gas.

The gas station attendant looks her way as he fills a red sports car, the driver following suit; they look up and down her body and their eyes speak of recognition, as though they were all meant to be here at this moment on this day.

Is she expected to be somewhere, other than here?

Frustration descends. Too many pulls in too many directions. She walks on, hoping she isn't screwing anything up.

The seagulls on the roof of the grocery store scream her back to her plan. Foodland. Brownies. Deborah's. It comes back to her in real time with toddlers holding hands, walking across the parking lot with their mothers who are weighed down with bags while the heat rises from the asphalt surface and an elderly man comes out of the store and shields his eyes against the burden of the midday sun. A simple pair of sunglasses would work well for him, she thinks, the sun behind her resting on her back, the clanking of grocery carts crashing in on her ears.

She grabs a basket, in case she comes across other things she might need, and enters the store and the tubes of light on the ceiling pain her eyes and the aisles of choice overwhelm and disturb and *hush, come now* from Buddy Francis's face as it lies among bread and pastries and at the tips of the fingers of her own hand picking up a package of brownies while the lights melt into the crease of her forehead and she spots an apple pie for dessert later at her own house — later when she goes home and faces the music of her sudden disappearance into the smoke of a cigarette and freshly cut lawn, past dog shit and farmers, turning right like the transport past the bulk food and pigeon shit and the rolling numbers on the gas pump, landing here at Foodland where what she chooses to buy seems as important as everything else today.

She walks with an unglued sensation to the cash and the approaching transaction is hinging on her ability to relieve one hand from the handles of the basket and dig into her pocket for the money and it is disconcerting to think this must be slowed down in order to happen. She can't move fast now. She fixes her eyes on the rack of chocolate bars, counting off in her head all the ones she has tried in her life and her all-time favourites, thinking that this is important, she doesn't know how or why, but it is, it just is. Oh Henry. Crunchie. Sweet Marie.

"I'll help you now, Natha," says Carol the cashier. Carol with her weathered, drinking, smoking, fifty-something face.

"Sorry," Natha says.

Oh, to move about town at a time like this when the air is thick with details — the creases in the plastic bag, dirt streaks on the floor, and the felt knowledge that others see her making her loose way out of the store into the parking lot, lighting another cigarette and inhaling the importance in all of this, vowing not to fail to see all that collectively stamps this day.

Another seagull scream punctuates her resolve and it is no surprise that, when the idea of going to Ruthie's first pops into her mind, she simply yields to it and crosses the street on the side of the liquor store. Several cars pull into the lot and she walks on, ignoring the impulse to buy a bottle. But the taste is with her now and so, yes, when Ruthie offers one upon her arrival, a glass of red wine would be nice.

And a cigarette, of course, on the balcony.

"Brownies and red wine and a good friend," Ruthie says. "What more could an old broad want?"

"We can't eat them all," Natha tells her.

A red hummingbird hovers over the purple morning glories wound around the railing.

"I don't want to be poor," she says to Ruthie.

Ruthie lets out a long sigh.

"Standing in the grocery store with a couple of bucks for bread. Cheap bread. Looking at all the chocolate bars I'd like to buy for Celia but can't afford."

"I know, love."

"Shit. I bought one and it's probably melted now."

"Not having a good day?"

Natha can see Ruthie's eyes and mouth moving and she can understand every word she is saying about being on edge and it's normal when you're thinking of ending a marriage, she can hear her, and all of it makes sense, but Ruthie seems strangely unreal. She puts her cigarette out and lights another.

"You're smoking a lot."

"I just can't see my way out of it."

"It'll be tough, but you will."

"John said that too."

"He knows that too?"

"He knows everything. I told him. At least, I'm sure I told him. We were standing in the kitchen for a long time. I must have shut down. It's all coming back in bits and pieces. This getting closer to the truth is hard."

"What do you mean by truth? The truth of what, love?"

"Of everything," Natha answers. "I'm supposed to be somewhere. I have to go."

"Love, are you all right?"

"I'm fine. I just have to go."

She was hoping Ruthie would have something profound to say, telling her she's on the right track, that she's doing what she's supposed to be doing. But with only concern coming out of her mouth, Natha decides to leave the apartment. She makes her way to Deborah's. The licence plates on passing cars buzz with meaning in her mind — LUVS U2 — reassuring her that the day so far has not been wasted.

As she turns the corner to Deborah's street, a large cloud eclipses the sun and, in the shade of What Comes Next, she decides she must call Irene and ask her if what she said yesterday is what she thought she said. Then she'll know for sure if this is all real.

When she gets to Deborah's, she asks to use the phone and calls her mother.

"Tell me what you told me the other day," she says to Irene.

"I don't want to go over that again," Irene replies, letting out a long and weary sigh.

"So it did happen, like you said, with Buddy Francis, with Daddy there drunk and passing out."

"Quit calling him Daddy!" Irene shouts. "He was no good for nothing."

"He knew then? You're sure he knew?"

"Let it go, dear. Let it go."

"I *need* to know," Natha says as forcefully as she can while still keeping her voice lowered while Deborah is in the kitchen rummaging through a cupboard. She can hear the clanging of what she thinks are glasses.

Irene hesitates then finally answers. "That's why I got him to leave."

"You didn't get him to leave. He left by his own choice."

"No, he didn't. Now, where are you Natha?"

"I have to go. I can't believe you knew all along that it happened and you never did anything. Not a goddamn thing."

"Everything okay?" Deborah asks, walking back into the living room with two teacups and saucers. Natha hangs up on her mother, sets the phone back down.

"Fine. This will help."

She can smell the liquor before the cup lands in her hands.

"This isn't tea."

"Scotch. This is my way of having the ladies in for tea. You seemed so upset yesterday. Believe me, I know how it feels when you accidentally hurt your child. I once elbowed Amber right in the eye."

"Imagine what it's like for someone who intentionally hurts a child. I mean, you have to feel something, don't you?"

"Not if you're a sociopath."

Is that what Buddy Francis is? Christ, she was Celia's age. The question sits on the rim of her cup and becomes more likely with every sip and she takes huge gulps to coat her mouth. She notices a chip in the side of the cup and thinks it must be old. It looks old, blue and gold, and the white inside dull now.

"I see you didn't sell all your cups and saucers you had at the yard sale."

"We still have a ton of them."

Christ, Natha thinks. It can't be.

"Is your mother here?" she asks, nonchalantly.

"In her room, reading. She's always been an avid reader. We have a ton of books too, from before she became blind. If you read you can take some home."

"I have plenty. What's your mother's name?"

"Christina," Deborah answers.

Natha swallows hard on her next sip and she feels as if she's just been hit with a heavy stone. But she hides the discovery. There's the question of Deborah's younger sister. She knows who she looks like now.

"So," Natha says. "Your mother collected cups and saucers?"

"And books. She loved them just as much."

"Books. I see. Tell you what. I really need to go someplace. Could you pick Celia up and bring her back here with you. I won't be long."

"Absolutely, but I'll need a note for the teacher to let me do that."

"Of course. Do you have a pen and paper?"

"Is it something I said?" Deborah asks, not understanding this sudden need to leave.

"Not at all. You just made me think of someone I need to see."

THE SKY HAS GONE grey. The wind has picked up; it pushes her up the hill on Henry Street. There's no second-guessing herself anymore. Everything she thought was real is real, and then some. She knows now that a child was born by Christina Reid and that it was Jack Callaberry's child. Stacey looks just like her sister, Mary, John Gulliver's wife, and they both look like Jack. What to do with it all? Her head is swimming and she can hardly feel her feet beneath her.

John didn't make up the story and he didn't make up the things he said to her. With this, she knocks on Jules's door.

"Back again already? Come in, come in."

He is wearing only a light housecoat.

"Don't bother with the drinks this time," she tells him, taking her usual spot in the wingback chair. He rests his back against the couch. It all seems so dull now, the house. But she decides she wants the bookcases and all the books, and the one Royal Doulton figurine. As far as she's concerned they belong to her.

"I want money," she says, flatly.

"Well, you have to earn it," Jules replies, grinning. "I have an idea how you can do that."

"Always the games, Jules."

"You need money, and I have it, Natha. What better arrangement could there be than that."

"The only thing I'll do is keep secret what you did to me, let you die with your reputation intact."

"What I did to you? I didn't do anything to you you didn't want."

"I was fifteen, Jules."

"You were wise beyond your years."

"You're a rapist and you know it."

"I loved you, Natha. Tell me what you know about love."

"If you loved me, then I don't have to tell you what love is or isn't. You already know."

"Now who's playing games?"

Jules stands up and makes his way to his desk.

"Make it a big cheque. I earned it."

"I'll write the cheque but I didn't rape anyone."

From her chair, Natha sees the Royal Doulton figurine in the hutch. She walks over to it and takes it from the shelf.

"I'm taking this, too," she says, then stops beside his desk.

Jules hands her the cheque. From where she stands, towering over him, he looks small and harmless.

"Just tell me how you feel about me dying. Can you do that?"

His blue eyes meet hers and he waits for her answer.

She could tell him that what she feels is a kind of rage that has been there all these years, the kind of rage that makes you feel like a fly buzzing around in a lampshade unable to move on. That the rage separated her from her body, a rage that only her mind could control. But what would be the point of letting him know that? Besides, the rage must have started before that — back with Buddy Francis.

Can a young girl feel rage?

Jules will be dead someday soon, she thinks

He'll be gone.

"I can only tell you that I don't feel anything resembling love," she says, then walks out of the house, closing the door hard behind her. She just makes it down the front steps when the door is opened.

"Just tell me it isn't hatred you feel," he calls out. He repeats it again, but his plaintive tone does not make her break her stride. She walks on, this time into the wind, back to Deborah's, stopping in long enough to get her daughter and head home. She gives the figurine to Celia, who is happy to get a present. She holds it with both hands as she walks home. She asks if she can call her "Rosy Red."

"That's a great name," Natha tells her. Even if the china girl is dropped and broken, Natha still feels like she's rescued it just by getting it out of Jules' house. Even in pieces, it would be free. The analogy doesn't go unnoticed. A broken, fallen woman can still think straight.

SIXTEEN

IT HAPPENS ON A grey morning with an inward sky, the heat of summer bleeding into September. As she gets Celia ready for school, Natha hears a robin. She watches the clouds move at a fast pace as they head down Edward Street to Mill Street, past Ren's restaurant and the old Stedman's store. With the welcoming storefronts, the town feels to Natha like a stage set, theatrical and unreal.

She awoke with a feeling that today would be the day she begins to write in earnest, after months of making notes; she feels the rush upside her back, which is knotless now, at ease, willing to bend into the task ahead. As she showered and got dressed, she imagined her fingers at the keyboard of her computer.

She knows the writing will have to wait. There is something she has to do before she can begin to tell her story. "Just wait," she whispers to the stirring along her spine. "Just wait."

IN ANOTHER PART OF town, on Henry Street, at the top of the hill, John Gulliver is getting ready for a sale. Natha kisses Celia goodbye at school and makes her way there. The past two months wind and unwind in her mind like a reel of film.

It would be a silent film, Natha thinks as she remembers the previous summer as a series of long, hot days, sifting into one another, a blanket of the unknown sheathing her, protecting her, demanding that she let go. The woman in her head has all but disappeared; she hadn't heard her so much as experienced her as a memory. Natha no longer feels there is something outside of herself, something narrating her steps, lending meaning to the objects in her house. Celia's small silver crown is simply a child's toy, not a sign; the birth rock simply an egg-shaped rock, not a marker of rebirth. Whatever it was that shaded her world, that lent meaning to things, has retreated, leaving the stark reality that things are just as they appear.

She moves through town, a stranger to most, going about her business. There is no force telling her to turn right, to make a left, to avoid Henry Street. The gas station attendant barely sees her, the items in the store are inanimate and mute.

She doesn't know what happened to her in the lifting, linking days of June but it is all gone now. Ruthie told her it was like she was trapped by something, something she couldn't articulate.

"No. Trapped isn't the word," Ruthie said. "That would imply someone did it to you. Or that you did it to yourself. No, it was more like you were a leaf, carried by the wind, dropped on water, and then frozen underneath the ice of the pond."

Whatever it was, Natha couldn't push herself beyond it.

Dr. David Riddell answered her last email about her ability to push herself beyond everything and said, "It's not so much that you push beyond your present as it is that you suspend belief and your place in reality, and ultimately believe nothing is happening to you."

But she did believe in everything — until it all went away.

What made it go away?

The obvious answer is John Gulliver. He didn't call, didn't come around. Week after week, there was no word from him. She tried to remember the things he had said, but only a few stood out as real, something she could be sure he said. The notes she had been making, the ones that led to her writing, were her memories of what she thought had taken place between them.

She strained to remember any of what he said. The phrases she did remember, like "Come fly away with me," she knows now weren't real. His words started to break up into pieces, then to dust, then nothing.

But before then, the memories and the reason for the memories were going away. When she returned home that day with Celia carrying Rosy Red, after she had left Deborah's, after she left Jules's place with the cheque, she got home and Devon was Devon, blasting her for her irresponsibility for running off that day to go to a friend's whom he had never heard about. How was it that she had a friend he knew nothing about? How did that feed their marriage? He didn't act like someone who was willing to let her go.

But it was before that, when Celia didn't drop Rosy Red

on the way home, when the figurine didn't break and end up in pieces. Natha walked into the house, looked around, and realised that nothing had any meaning. The clock on the wall was quiet and unthreatening.

Just before she fell asleep that night, Celia sang "Baby-loves-the-Mama" to Natha. She was holding Rosy Red and thanking Natha for giving it to her. The only thing that had any meaning to Natha that night was her daughter's young child hands wrapped around that china girl. It was like they were Natha's own six-year-old hands.

By late July, Natha asked Devon to move out. He did, reluctant and angry. She offered to help him pay for an apartment; she was willing to withdraw some money from her Come What May Account, but he moved in with Barb. She didn't need to finance that situation.

"I can come back, you know. Once you get over whatever this is. Barb knows where the line is drawn, that you're my wife. I can see you're just messed up right now."

She let it go at that, let him think what he wanted. She felt clear-minded about her decision. It was John Gulliver's words, the real ones, *I could never share you*. She knows he said that. They weren't part of the breaking words.

But still, no word from John. It seemed as if it never happened, even though she knows she sat on a picnic table with John at King's Mill; they had walked down the road past Christina's old house. He had been in Natha's house, standing in the kitchen, in his white shirt and jeans, leaning against her white cupboards.

She had read the ads for his auction sales in the newspaper, but didn't attend them. Had she really imagined a relationship where one hadn't been? In early August, she thought she saw his black truck driving past the house on Edward Street, then again when she was sitting on a stump in the tall grasses beside the Mill Pond, watching two herons perched on a large rock. She was moved by the sight of them. Rarely had she seen two together. When the black truck passed a second time, she was sure it was John who had caught sight of her. He didn't stop to talk to her. She was left with that brief presence of him, with the story of Jack and Christina, with the secret life of objects.

After the day at the Mill Pond, she was left with the news of Jules's death. Ruthie told Natha that they found him dead in his bed. He had taken an overdose of pills, left no explanation, only instructions for his assets to be auctioned. It made Natha think of Jack Callaberry. She decided to give some of Jules's money to Deborah for her family. It seemed only fitting, given what she knew about Jack Callaberry and Christina and Deborah's sister, Stacey. She told Deborah the day she delivered the cheque that she wouldn't explain the windfall. All Deborah needed to know was that Natha hadn't robbed a bank.

She sees now the straight lines that have led to this freedom, how the memories have fallen into place. As the summer unfolded, Natha began to make notes about what John had or hadn't said; Devon playing his guitar and her not feeling anything; Celia's birth; Jules with a copy of *Lolita* in his hands; the brawny boys with hay bales; Sketchy Woman lying bare and waiting to be played with. She made notes about the reeking walls of the rooms at the Sunrise enclosing her. Jack and Christina. Cups and saucers.

It may just be the inward sky today that encourages her to walk along Henry Street towards the auction sale at Jules's house. Whatever it is, Natha feels the need to see John. To look into his eyes, which she knows can't lie.

He is standing in the backyard when she arrives, looking over Jules's collection of figurines. At first he doesn't see her approaching, but she steps on a twig, which snaps, and he looks her way. Two guys are at the other end of the yard putting Jules's hutch in place. John steps towards her when he sees her. She approaches slowly and meets his eyes. He stands, says nothing, his eyes taking her in.

"I couldn't do it," he says.

She thinks she sees tears in his eyes, just like she saw that day at King's Mill.

"I just couldn't do it," he repeats. It's his plea for her to understand.

She sees past him to the neat rows of Jules's furniture and tables of dishes. She can see that he never did say anything about flying away together. He is grounded here, selling off the goods of a dead man, his wife collecting the money.

"I know," she says to him. "I just had to come."

"I look for you at all the sales," he tells her. "It's like you just disappeared."

"I could say the same about you."

She decides there's no point in telling him about Christina being back in town or about Jack's other daughter, Stacey.

"I might come to a sale one day," she says. "But not for a very long time."

As she turns to leave, he reaches for her arm.

"I can't have something that real," he says. "But you can, Natha. And I hope you do."

He tries to smile.

Natha leaves Jules's backyard, walks away from the house. A chapter has closed in her life. As she walks back, down Henry Street, she feels the warm thaw of herself.

Maybe there will be someone to love someday, someone who will love her.

Love can enter now.

She'll write those words down when she gets home, but she knows that it is the end of the story, not the beginning. The right words to start the story elude her now.

She doesn't know how long she'll have the freedom of her days and nights to write, or what she'll do when she sees Buddy Francis again, or how she really feels about Jules dying. At least he gave her the money. He gave her the words, too, to tell the story, whatever they may be. All she knows for sure is that the longing she felt in the breaking words was real — the longing to believe they were real — and she'll write towards that.

It is still early in the morning, the town's shops are still locked. As she walks past the feed mill, she feels Daddy and the loss of him. She feels Irene's pain that Natha no longer needed her after the age of six. She feels the sweetness of John Gulliver brushing her hair out of her face.

She feels.

Back home, she catches sight of herself in the hallway mirror, her long, dark hair slightly messy from the breeze outside. She straightens it, trying to decide if she should put it up today or not. Devon always used to put it up. She decides to leave it down and heads upstairs to change into her bathing suit. She's in need of a swim, to relax. Maybe the words will come.

Standing in front of the full-length mirror in her bedroom, she can't help but think of the day so long ago when Daddy came into her room and saw her in her bra and underwear and told her she was filling out nicely. How she must have looked then, at the age of fourteen, with her young flesh, not yet touched by Jules. Standing there, she can feel herself inside her body, can feel its years of usage, and yet it remains the same. Even her hair is the same, which has been stroked and pulled and pinned up by countless men. That's when it comes —

She takes the scissors she cuts Celia's hair with and begins to cut her own, the long, dark hair surrounding her face. She cuts her hair short, just above the neckline, the place where her head is separated from her body. The shanks fall to the floor, fall with the weight of the years living outside of her own body, outside of herself. *Tell me what you know about love*, Jules said.

She continues to cut her hair. She cannot answer.

What does she know about love?

Jules said he loved her. Devon did too. Daddy said it a few times that she remembers. Irene never did. She thinks of John Gulliver, brushing her hair from her face, how loving the gesture felt. And Jack and Christina, a love that killed. She rounds the back of her head, cutting by feel only, not caring if she makes a straight line or a jagged one, only caring that the weight comes off. She may not know much about love, but with the last of her hair falling to the floor, she feels a possibility she hasn't felt before, standing in front of the mirror, looking different, looking ahead.

SHE SWIMS OUT FROM the beach across the lake from her mother's house, swims out past the raft, without the weight of long wet hair on her back. It may take a while to get used to the short hair that was born this morning. It may take a while to get used to a new life.

She swims hard, feeling the strength in her arms, her legs; the strength of her body, a body that is once again her own. When the phone rings next, she will tell them to find someone else, she has moved on. In the middle of the small lake she stops to tread water, to catch her breath, to catch a million thankful breaths. She can see a figure on the lawn at her mother's house and she knows it is Irene, taking her first drink of the day. For a moment, Natha considers going the distance, swimming to the other side. But she turns instead and begins to head back. A light rain is starting. She's got work to do. The words can enter now.

ACKNOWLEDGEMENTS

I was fortunate enough to have emotional and creative support over the years of writing, and I wish to thank the following people whose generous spirits often kept me going: Gerry Fraiberg, Steve Heighton, Colleen Mitchell, Lori Kennedy Silverthorne and Dr. Paul Zimmerman.

I am indebted to Lindy Powell and Denyse Mouck for deep friendship and loyalty, and to Kalie, for insightful, soulful conversation and for sharing the ride.

I am grateful to live between two pillars of strength — my mother, Elizabeth, and my daughter, Anna, who never lost faith in me.

I thank everyone at Cormorant Books for their contribution, and especially, Marc Côté for editorial guidance and for believing in Natha and her story.

With appreciation for assistance from The Canada Council for the Arts and the Ontario Arts Council for a much earlier draft of this novel, then under a different title.